IF A CHURCH PEW COULD TALK

PRAISE FOR IF A CHURCH PEW COULD TALK

Wow! The book, *If a Church Pew Could Talk*, by author Cindy Carraway Williams is such an amazing story and a must read! The book shares stories of three families that will make you laugh, cry, and be inspired multiple times throughout this book. The stories in Cindy's book are extremely engaging and make you feel that you are right there with these families and living this journey yourself in real time. It was so encouraging to see God work in the lives of these members of Pumpkin Creek United Church. Although we do not understand His ways (Proverbs 3:5), God works His plan in His time for His glory. And this book showed God at work throughout the journey. To God be the Glory. We highly recommend this book.

—**Mark and Ginger Whitacre**, National Keynote Speakers (Mark Whitacre, VP Culture and Care and Executive Director of Coca-Cola Consolidated. The book, *The Informant*, and the movie by the same name are based on Mark Whitacre's life as a Federal Bureau of Investigation whistleblower).

Get ready for a fascinating journey back through the lives, loves, and losses of a handful of families at a small eastern North Carolina community church. Each chapter of *If a Church Pew Could Talk*, highlights the impact of local and national historical events through the unique observations of a fixture of the church—an old oak pew! You'll love it!

—**Pastor Robert Kornegay**, Emerald Isle Chapel By The Sea

If a Church Pew Could Talk is a delightful historical tale of a church pew spanning over a hundred and fifty years. The tales Everett shares, the insights into church life, and the personalities the pew watches made me laugh and cry. You may even see yourself in the pages, alongside some historical figures. I thoroughly enjoyed this story and came away with the following quotes echoing in my mind. "His ways and His plans are not always our ways." (Joseph) "In my opinion, certain scars have great stories behind them." (Everett the pew) "Because God knows all." (Everett the pew)

—**Donna K. Stearns**, pastor's wife, Bible teacher, and author of *The Nazarene's Price*

Far from typical, *If a Church Pew Could Talk* is an interesting twist on stories about those we meet in church. Readers are taken on a journey spanning decades as told from the perspective of one of the church's original pews. Family ties are woven throughout the church's history bringing a richness to the story and creating a sense of nostalgia as readers consider their own church history. The good, the bad, and the ugly are all given space in the telling. And, let's be real, there is plenty of each of those making up the history of every church. *If a Church Pew Could Talk* goes beyond entertainment, though it is that too. The book is a reminder to reflect on our own faith roots and learn from the stories we find there.

—**Heather Greer**, author, speaker, pastor's wife

If a Church Pew Could Talk is a wonderful story of Everett that spans more than a century. You won't be able to put down this book. The unique story full of historical events will make you laugh often and cry a few times too.

—**Larry J. Leech II**, writing coach of award-winning authors

IF A CHURCH PEW COULD TALK

CINDY CARRAWAY WILLIAMS

Copyright © 2023 by Cindy Carraway Williams

Printed in the United States of America

All rights reserved. No part of this publication may be reproduced in any form or by any electronic or mechanical means, including information storage and retrieval systems, without prior written permission from the author, except for the use of brief quotations in printed reviews.

For permission requests:
Cindy Carraway Williams
https://www.cindycarrawaywilliams

Paperback ISBN: 979-8-9892584-0-6

Cover design and interior formatting by *Hannah Linder Designs*
www.hannahlinderdesigns.com

Some Scripture taken from the King James Version of the Bible. Public domain.

Some Scripture taken from the (NASB®) New American Standard Bible®, Copyright © 1960, 1971, 1977, 1995 by The Lockman Foundation. Used by permission. All rights reserved. www.lockman.org.

This book is a work of fiction. Any references to historical events, real people, or real places are used fictitiously. Other names or characters, businesses or places, events or incidents are drawn from the author's imagination. Any resemblance to actual events, places, organizations, locales, or persons, living or dead, is entirely coincidental.

For all the church pews tossed aside for chairs

IF A CHURCH PEW COULD TALK
FAMILY TREES

Thatcher Family

Pastor John Everett Thatcher (b. 1819)
married to Mary Lewis Thatcher (b. 1820)

John and Mary Thatcher's Children (4)

1. John Michael Thatcher (b. 1838)
married to Elizabeth Harris Thatcher (b. 1840)
John Michael and Elizabeth Thatcher's Child
John Michael Thatcher (known as Little John, b. 1860)

2. Esther Mary Thatcher (b. 1840)

3. Sarah Thatcher (b. 1846)

4. Joseph Everett Thatcher (b. 1842)
married to Kay Wilson Thatcher (b. 1846)
Joseph and Kay Thatcher's Children (6)

(1) Amos John Thatcher (b. 1868)
married to Anna Moore Thatcher (b. 1868)
Amos and Anna Thatcher's Children (3)
Suzy Thatcher (b. 1888)
Deborah Thatcher (b. 1890)
Lizzie Thatcher (b. 1891)

(2) Edward Thatcher (b. 1872)
married to Rebecca Price Thatcher (b. 1875–d. 1904)
Edward Thatcher married
Laura White Thatcher (b. 1879) in 1908.
Edward and Rebecca Thatcher's Children (3)
James Thatcher (b. 1899)
Luke Thatcher (b. 1901)
Martha Thatcher (b. 1904)

James Thatcher married Ethel Watson Thatcher (b. 1901)
James and Ethel Thatcher's Children (4)
Katie Thatcher (b. 1922)
Floyd Owen Thatcher (b. 1927)
John Luke Thatcher (b. 1932)
Ethel Louise Thatcher (b. 1938)

(3) Paul Thatcher (b. 1873)
married to Alice Dawson Thatcher (b. 1875)
Paul and Alice Thatcher's Children (2)
Claire Thatcher (b. 1899)
Ezekiel Thatcher (b. 1905)

(4) Mary Beth Thatcher (b. 1875)

(5) Naomi Thatcher (b. 1877)

(6) Ruth Thatcher (b. 1880)

Ward Family

Obadiah Ward (b. 1842) married to Sarah Hall Ward (b. 1846)

Obadiah and Sarah Ward's Child
Benjamin Obadiah Ward (b. 1872)
married to Suzanne Jackson Ward (b. 1874)

Benjamin Obadiah and Suzanne Ward's Child
Jackson Benjamin Ward Sr. (b. 1913)
married to Helen Smith Ward (b. 1914)

Jackson Benjamin (Sr.) and Helen Ward's Child
Jackson Benjamin Ward Jr. (b. 1940)
married to Carolyn Taylor Ward (b. 1943)

Jackson Benjamin (Jr.) and Carolyn Ward's Child
Bennett Carl Ward (b. 1965)
married to Roberta Davis Ward (b. 1967)

Bennett and Roberta Ward's Child
John Bennett Ward (known as Junior and b. 1991)
married to Rachel Nicole Robinson (b. 1992)

Wilson Family

Amos Wilson (b. 1821)
married to Cora Packard Wilson (b. 1824)

Amos and Cora Wilson's Children (3)
Emma Wilson (b. 1842)
Polly Wilson (b. 1844)
Kay Wilson (b. 1846)
(Kay married Joseph Everett Thatcher)

Pumpkin Creek United Church Pastors

1852–1874 John Everett Thatcher
1874–1884 John Michael Thatcher
1884–1885 Traveling Preachers
1885–1893 Claude Wentworth
1893–1895 Traveling Preachers
1895–1918 Jeremiah Johnston
1919–1926 Reverend Doyle
1926–1941 Preacher Rowe
1941–1965 Pastor Dunn
1965–1967 Preacher Poythress
1968–1973 Dr. Luther
1973–1990 Bill Boseman
1990–2011 "Reverend" (Randall Freeman)
2011–2023 Pastor Lee

CONTENTS

1. Present Day: No Place Like Home — 1
2. 1854: A Pew is Born — 13
3. 1865: An Encounter with General Sherman — 25
4. 1882: A Man After God's Own Heart — 41
5. 1899: Times are Changin' — 51
6. 1908: Becoming Mrs. Thatcher — 61
7. 1919: A Veteran's Burden — 75
8. 1927: Floyd "Fast-Hand" Owens — 89
9. 1933: The Night the Devil Came to Church — 109
10. 1949: A Pig Named Bar-B-Que — 123
11. 1955: God Knows What's Under Your Hat and in Your Heart — 133
12. 1967: Corned Beef Hash — 145
13. 1973: The Mischievous Papa Pat — 159
14. 1986: Troy's Gone Fishin' — 173
15. 1999: The Funeral of Juicy Fruit Jay — 185
16. 2004: You've Been Left Behind — 195
17. 2013: God's Plan for Billy Williams — 205
18. Current Day: Everett's New Home — 215

Acknowledgments — 225
About the Author — 229

1

PRESENT DAY: NO PLACE LIKE HOME

*D*espite being here for a century and a half, my future now hangs in the balance. I hope these church members do right by me and my friends.

One lady suggests replacing me with chairs. Chairs! The woman, and her cohorts, cannot be serious.

Tempers rise. I am stuck—bolted to the floor halfway back on the left-hand side. For now.

You see, as a pew, I have all the time in the world, and I am knowledgeable of all happenings in our sanctuary. Thousands of humans have graced our church with their presence. Over the decades, I have heard folks whisper and gossip forgetting God hears their words as do I. The tall, pitched ceiling above the chandeliers, along with oak pews and other solid furniture, cause sound to resonate. I get an earful.

I hear all sorts of prayer requests—a child with cancer, financial burdens over the loss of a job, or an adult child battling addiction. I also hear people argue over the silliest things.

Who would fathom choosing the color of carpet would

cause division among church folks? Once carpet became popular, our wood floors were covered. Of course, our church is quite old, and periodically, the original wood planks were replaced because they bent, sagged, or cracked. Members and visitors put much wear and tear on our wood floors with high heels, stomping feet, and all those folks who make their way down the aisle each week to stanzas of "Just As I Am" to kneel at the altar and confess their sins, a number of transgressions I am not willing to repeat.

Now, I reside upon gray carpet. Boring, if you ask me.

However, today, our members' vote is not about carpet. The vote is about me and the other thirty-nine pews.

I hear chairs are more fashionable, but I cannot imagine Pumpkin Creek United Church without pews. The church is located near the river outside the small town of Greenville, North Carolina, two miles down Pumpkin Creek Road. The church has been here since before the thunderous night back in 1854 when I was struck by lightning, hauled to the sawmill, and pounded and sanded into the church pew that I am.

"Now, now." Fifty-year-old Pastor Lee, trim from all the running he does, pushes his rimless eyeglasses up further on his nose. He bangs a gavel against the lectern. Members, who remained after the Sunday morning service for the business meeting, quiet down their rising voices. "We'll have a discussion, then vote." The pastor places the gavel on the pulpit. "We must follow Robert's Rules of Order."

"Amen," an elderly gentleman says.

"Let's begin with a recap of what is proposed, and then have a discussion." The pastor looks at Roberta Ward, the most well-dressed woman in the church. She's known in the circles of the church ladies as Mrs. Highfalutin'.

Roberta stands and presses her hands down the front of her

skirt. "These pews are old-fashioned, and the time to remove them is now."

Uh-oh. Roberta's late husband, Bennett, was the epitome of the strong, silent type and a God-fearing man. I miss him, as do most people here. Bennett always reined Roberta in on her tactless behavior. Without him, my fellow pews and I are in trouble.

"They've been here since the doors to our church opened." Ethel Louise's eighty-five-year-old voice is gentle, yet strained. "My great-great-grandfather, Pastor John Everett Thatcher, had that pew"—she stands, turns facing the aisle, and points at me—"created to honor what God did in healing my great-grandfather." Ethel Louise focuses on an older man. "Max, please read the plaque attached on the armrest. Maybe we'll be reminded of our history."

I adopted my name, Everett, after Pastor Thatcher's youngest son, Joseph Everett Thatcher, an upright, godly man if ever there was one.

"Yes, ma'am." Max stands in the aisle, faces the small plaque, and squints his eyes behind reading glasses. "With God, all things are possible. Joseph Everett Thatcher. Healed of yellow fever, 1854. To God be the glory." Max steps back into the row and sits.

"Good grief, Ethel. We're all familiar with the history of our church and the pew." Mrs. Highfalutin' arches her high brows further up. "Several other pews have plaques attached in honor or memory of someone too."

"Now, ladies, we have a wonderful history at our church." Pastor Lee smiles and addresses Ethel Louise. "You and the Ole Holy Ladies do a wonderful program each year at our homecoming service." He pauses and looks at Roberta a few extra seconds before he returns his attention to the others. "You ladies remind us of what God does when we stay focused on Him and faithful to His Word."

"Let's vote," Mrs. Highfalutin's sharp tone indicates her displeasure. "Five years ago, when we did our renovations, we should have removed these old things. If we don't place the order this coming week, the chairs will not be here in time for our Easter service. In a manner of speaking, our big reveal."

"Hold on," the preacher holds up a hand, "let's finish the discussion."

"At the time of the renovation," Max gives Roberta a hard look, "we were over budget, and more projects weren't feasible. We updated the sound system here in the sanctuary, added Smart TVs and electronics in our Sunday school classes, remodeled all four bathrooms, and repainted the church and fellowship hall where needed. We did all we could afford."

"Nancy, Donna Rae, and I have done all the legwork." Irritation sounds in Roberta's voice. "The prototype the manufacturer sent us has been on display in the fellowship hall for a few weeks now, and we've placed the chair up front with a fabric sample." Roberta acknowledges Nancy with the go-ahead. Roberta and Ethel Louise sit. Nancy walks over and stands beside the chair, lifts the fabric sample, and motions with her hands in exaggerated gestures.

"Who does she think she is?" A teenager snickers. "A model from *The Price is Right?*"

"Okay, Nancy." Roberta nods, and Nancy returns to her seat. "You all have seen the chair and fabric, what's the holdup?" Mrs. Highfalutin' looks at Ethel Louise.

This lady is ready to kick me from my home. I realize I am old and scarred. I have been bumped into with the machine called a vacuum cleaner countless times. Babies and toddlers have vomited on me. Children have marked me with crayons and ink pens, and I cannot begin to explain how much gum is stuck to the bottom of my seat. What will become of me if I am tossed from my home? I cannot become a tree again.

"What will we do with all these pews?" Ethel Louise frowns.

Oh, thank you, Miss Ethel Louise. You read my thoughts.

"Who'd want them?" Nancy taps her pink-polished forefinger nail against her lip. Her movement stops. "Maybe we donate them to a charity."

"Or burn them," Mrs. Highfalutin' mutters under her breath.

Burn us. All forty pews. Oh, please do not let that happen.

Ethel Louise purses her lips and shakes her head.

"I have an idea, Pastor." Max stands, and Roberta frowns at him. "We all agree, our church has a long history, and though we have made updates inside and out over the years, we've kept pieces that were too expensive to replace or didn't fit into the budget at the time." He finds the church secretary sitting on the front pew and recording the business meeting minutes. "Tammy, don't we still have records going back to when the church was built?"

Tammy twists in her seat and faces Max. "Yes, I believe we do. Why?"

"How about if Miss Ethel Louise, you, and I do research? Contact folks in the community and the historical society, and see what options are out there for saving the pews."

"That's a wonderful idea, Max." Tammy grins.

"Splendid." Ethel Louise smiles and nods.

Yes, the best idea I have ever heard. Please save me.

"I agree." Pastor Lee looks from Tammy to Max to Ethel Louise. "We have time. Once we place the order for the chairs, if we have a unanimous vote, they'll arrive in about four weeks."

Satisfied, Max sits back down, crosses suit-clad legs, and folds sturdy arms over his chest.

"I have a few documents at my house." Ethel Louise holds her head high. "Maybe we could find descendants of the original church parishioners, like me."

"Now you're grasping at straws." Roberta's voice drips with disdain. "They're probably all dead."

Nancy and Donna Rae gasp at the audacity of their friend's words. Ethel Louise's face drops.

Mrs. Highfalutin' ignores them. "We have to get with the program, update with the times. You old folks are making the vote on chairs harder than necessary."

"Excuse me," Max interrupts, "because we're older doesn't make us useless."

Oh my, Mrs. Highfalutin' Roberta Ward needs a kick on the backside of the designer dress she's wearing—to hurt Ethel Louise's feelings and all the other elderly folks who attend the church. Miss Ethel Louise is an older member—or an old maid to some—but she has served our church and our community. Dedicating her life to the education of her students for close to forty years, she retired and volunteered her time as a mentor to teachers at the local high school. Not to mention all the Sunday school classes she has taught here and the encouragement and support she provides others, in particular the sick and shut-ins. Roberta's only contribution has been to cause disharmony among members.

"Roberta, please." Donna Rae groans.

"The church has been here for over one hundred and fifty years." A deep crease forms between Pastor Lee's eyebrows. He directs a gaze toward Roberta. "Our church survives through God's grace and Him allowing us to do His will."

"Amen," a deacon calls out.

"You all, let us remember, 'Thou shalt rise up before the hoary head, and honour the face of the old man, and fear thy God ...' Leviticus nineteen, verse thirty-two," Max quotes without opening a Bible. "For all you youngsters, hoary means white, silvered. See my hair." He pats the top of his head.

"Pastor, I'm not following Robert's Rule of Order"—an Ole Holy Lady interjects—"but I'm going to read a few verses. Turn in your Bibles to Titus chapter two and starting with verse two."

Members flip pages in their Bibles. Others grab their cellphones searching for the verse. Ethel Louise retrieves her Bible while Roberta Ward straightens her jacket collar and mumbles.

The Ole Holy Lady picks up where she left off. "'That the aged men be sober, grave, temperate, sound in faith, in charity, in patience.' This describes the men in our church."

"Yes," Pastor Lee agrees.

"Ethel Louise, why don't you read verses three through five?" The Ole Holy Lady nudges her friend in the arm.

Ethel Louise clears her throat. "'The aged women likewise, that they be in behaviour as becometh holiness, not false accusers, not given to much wine, teachers of good things; That they may teach the young women to be sober, to love their husbands, to love their children, To be discreet, chaste, keepers at home, good, obedient to their own husbands, that the word of God be not blasphemed.'"

Pastor Lee smiles at the older ladies. "You exemplify these verses, Miss Ethel Louise, along with your group of the Ole Holy Ladies. Thank you all for meeting here every Monday morning and praying over our congregation. We see your prayers answered."

"And thanks for the prayer shawls you ladies crochet and distribute among the sick. I have mine from my spell with pneumonia thrown over my recliner in my family room," another member adds.

Pastor Lee gazes over the members. "We should hold our older population up, show them the respect they deserve, and care for them in their old age." He looks at Ethel Louise and her friends. "You ladies live these verses, and that's one of hundreds of reasons I'm proud of you all."

The Ole Holy Ladies faces beam from ear to ear. Some members send Roberta Ward a hard glare.

Roberta grunts. At fifty-six, she will be Ethel Louise's age before she knows what hit her. One day she will see. How Bennett endured his marriage to Roberta is a mystery to me, and I am certain, to everyone in the church. He was the humble to her high-handedness, the calm to her callousness, and the quiet to her loudness. I have heard opposites attract, and those two were complete opposites. God in His power works in mysterious ways.

Max raises his hand, and the pastor acknowledges him.

"Since Miss Ethel Louise is a retired history teacher, she can take the lead and instruct Tammy and me on the steps needed, so maybe, we can save these pieces of our history. Meanwhile, perhaps we'll find a home somewhere in the church for a couple of the pieces, you know ... to add character."

"That's a great idea," another Ole Holy Lady remarks. "My daughter is an interior designer. I'll ask her for suggestions too."

"Oh, brother." Mrs. Highfalutin' rolls her eyes. "Anything old will ruin the new décor theme."

"Let's hope the pews and other pieces find homes or are recycled," Pastor Lee says.

"If not," Roberta adds in haste, "I'll rent a wood chipper, and we'll be done with them once and for all."

Wood chips? Yikes!

Nancy and Donna Rae whip around facing each other and frown over their friend's words. Ethel Louise draws a sharp breath inward. A pink blush tinges her cheeks.

Oh, Miss Ethel Louise, please save me.

Pastor Lee darts his eyes from one woman to another. "Let's get back to our discuss—"

"Excuse me, Pastor." With slow precision, Ethel Louise stands, turns, and faces Mrs. Highfalutin' with the eyes of everyone watching her. She points an index finger at her. "Roberta Ward, your behavior is unacceptable."

"I have never." Roberta's eyes fly wide open.

Uh-oh, this is getting good.

"Do you not understand your behavior here today? You are disrespectful to our pastor, the members, and to me. We're having an adult discussion about this project. We don't need your snide remarks." Ethel Louise places a hand on the pew in front of her seat.

"You tell her," Max adds.

"You can't talk to me that way." Roberta glares at Ethel Louise. "I give more money to the church than any of you."

Members gasp. Pastor Lee gives her the 'no you didn't say that' look.

"Roberta," Donna Rae pleads. Nancy shields her face with a hand.

"God doesn't care how much money you give." Ethel Louise places her free hand on her hip. "As a matter of fact, your money is from Bennett's family, the Ward family, and they never bragged about their tithes and offerings. Maybe you could learn a lesson from them."

Roberta's nostrils flare. "You're behind the times."

"Is that so?" Ethel Louise questions in her strictest teacher's voice, then adds, "You're acting like the south end of a donkey heading north."

Roberta gasps. Ethel Louise faces front and sits. Whispers, snickers, and giggles erupt across the audience.

"Oh no, she didn't," a teenager utters before his mother hushes him.

Roberta lurches up off the pew. She snatches her Bible and purse. "Nancy? Donna Rae? You coming?" Nancy continues to hide part of her face. Donna Rae turns away avoiding eye contact with her friend. Roberta's face hardens, and with a harsh voice, she snaps at her friends. "Judas." Roberta whips around, her head held high.

People twist and turn in their seats and watch Mrs. Highfalutin' march from the church, banging the door when she leaves. Good thing Bennett has gone on to heaven and their son, Junior, lives a two-hour drive away in Raleigh with his wife. Those men, godly and humble, would have been embarrassed by her actions.

Members exchange glances with each other. No one breathes a word until two middle-school-aged boys snicker. One blurts, "That was so awkward."

Once the words escape the boy's mouth, folks shift in their seats. Whispered voices and a few chuckles resonate among the pews. Pastor Lee raises a hand, and the congregation calms down.

Donna Rae lifts her hand and speaks after the pastor looks in her direction. "I apologize, Pastor. I didn't know Roberta was going to act so—"

"That's okay, Donna Rae. Nobody's perfect, and you were not acting the way Miss Ethel Louise implied Roberta was." He darts eyes over the members. "The Bible tells us we should speak the truth."

The teen boy snickers. "Miss Ethel Louise sure did."

Pastor Lee continues, "I believe we've all learned a lesson."

"Yep," Max speaks up, "those of us with age and white hair, you can't push us or our ideas aside."

The teen blurts, "Yeah, don't mess with the old folks."

"Old folks." Ethel Louise shifts in her seat, faces the teen, and gives him a sharp look. "You want me to come back there?"

"No, ma'am." The teen blushes until Miss Ethel Louise's face bursts into a huge grin. With an embellished motion, he swipes a hand over his brow. "Whew." He looks at the preacher. "The floor's all yours, Pastor Lee."

"Okay, is there any more discussion on the pew versus chair issue?"

"You know," a middle-aged man near the front stands, "despite her pushiness and shenanigans, Roberta is on the right track. Most churches you go into nowadays have chairs." The man sits.

Nancy raises a tentative hand. "And chairs are easily moved in and out of the sanctuary—especially when we need more room for weddings or Christmas plays."

Pastor Lee nods. "Good point. If the motion passes replacing our pews with chairs, Max, Tammy, and Miss Ethel Louise will work on seeking placement of the pews. Now, do I have a motion?"

"I make a motion," the same middle-aged man says, "to replace the pews with chairs."

Donna Rae slides a cautious glance at Ethel Louise before lifting her arm in the air. "I second."

"All those in favor, raise your hand."

Sixty-one members raise their hands. Seven members vote against, one of which is Ethel Louise. I knew she would not desert me. Fate is not on my side, and my pew life is near an end, unless the three-person committee performs a miracle.

The account of my creation passes from generation to generation among Pumpkin Creek United Church members—a story I have heard time and time again.

And what a time my life has been.

2

1854: A PEW IS BORN

God's thunderous storms frighten the bravest of men and me. Friday, the ninth of June, the heavens roar, and lightning crackles with sharp, burning arrows through the afternoon sky. The Thatcher family huddles in their home, and I am rooted to the spot in the front yard until God gives my life a new purpose.

Twelve-year-old Joseph Everett Thatcher lies at death's door—motionless, eyes closed, and breathing shallow. Rain pounds the Thatcher home. Strong winds howl around the corner of their house. In the distance, horses neigh with nervous energy.

"Dear God, save my boy." Pastor John Everett Thatcher hovers over Joseph's sunken figure.

The oldest son, John Michael, pokes a drenched head around the half-opened bedroom door swiping the dampness off his face with a sleeve. "We've finished all the chores. You and Mother need to eat."

Pastor Thatcher nods, but how do parents eat while they watch their youngest son slip away?

"I need more cool water." Mary picks up the pail that holds the damp cloth she uses to wet and place onto her son's forehead, hoping and praying Joseph's fever dies down. She slides around her eldest son, walks to the kitchen, and pumps more cool water into the pail.

"Esther, Sarah, and I will pray again." John Michael glances at the bed holding his younger brother. "May we come in and see Joseph before ..."

The pastor responds without turning toward John Michael. "Yellow fever. Doc said our family must remain quarantined. Please keep your sisters in the other room."

"Yes, sir." John Michael's head and shoulders drop.

If Pastor Thatcher had not taken his sons to the yearly meeting of the Baptist ministers in Wilmington, North Carolina, this would not have happened. Unbeknownst to travelers, an infected ship of passengers had made port one day prior. After spending the night in a local boarding house, the three Thatcher men made haste and headed home.

Mary had begged him to take care of their youngest son. Joseph, frail as a baby and toddler, did not have a strong appetite and caught colds more often than his brother or sisters. By God's grace, Joseph had grown to twelve years of age. God-willing, he would become a teenager before Christmas.

A loud crash and thud rattles the tiny house.

"What was that?" The pastor asks to no one in particular except his unconscious son. He wanders over to the side window in the room. Rain hits the glass. A limb blows across the yard and toward the side pasture. "Mary's rose garden will be destroyed."

Pastor Thatcher catches sight of a dark-clothed, one-armed figure running toward the house, struggling against the storm. "Amos? What is the man doing? I thought he was in South Carolina." The pastor turns back toward Joseph. "Father, give my boy strength. Please keep my family and the community safe." Pastor Thatcher swipes the tears from his eyes and turns toward the bedroom door.

Amos Wilson pounds on the front door until someone answers. "Where's the preacher and Joseph?"

"You shouldn't be here." John Michael steps aside for Amos to enter.

"We're keeping ourselves quarantined," Mary says. "If you don't catch the fever, you'll catch a cold from being out in the storm."

"I know. The preacher stayed with me when I had the accident with my arm. No one thought I was going to live through the night. I'm here for him and your family."

The foreman at the local sawmill, Amos had lost his left arm in an accident a couple of years ago and still works as hard as any man with two arms.

Mary looks at her daughter. "Esther, please get Amos a towel."

Amos takes the towel from Esther and wipes off before he follows Mary into the bedroom. Pastor Thatcher sits in a chair next to the bed watching over Joseph.

Amos squeezes the pastor's shoulder before he steps away and stands at the footboard. Mary wrings a cloth out in the cool pan of water and places the rag on Joseph's forehead. The pastor stares at Joseph—the slight rise and fall of Joseph's chest, the boy's only movement.

Their youngest daughter, Sarah, and Esther sing "Amazing Grace," the gentle words ringing throughout their four-room home. Tears escape down Mary's cheeks. The pastor holds Joseph's warm hand between trembling fingers.

"I have never felt as helpless as I do now." Deep lines crease Pastor Thatcher's face. "Any others sick, Amos?"

"Not that I've heard. Doc said you did the right thing by keeping your family out here."

"I'm thankful for that." He glances at Mary. Grief etches every line of her face. "I asked Doc not to come back. We need to prevent the spread of the fever the best we can."

Mary glances at Amos. "I thought you were at your niece's wedding."

"We headed that way. But ..."

"Yellow fever?" the pastor asks.

Amos nods and traces the bed covering with his right index finger. "As we neared the coast, we met folks on the road. They said things didn't look good. I turned around. Didn't want our family at risk."

A blast ricochets outside, shaking a framed picture hanging on the wall behind Mary, who places her hand over her heart. Esther and Sarah stop singing. Sarah whimpers. Esther utters words and consoles her younger sister.

"Amos," the pastor requests of his friend, "please pray over my boy."

Pastor Thatcher knows whatever he asks of Amos, an elder at their church, will be done. The man lives a life on the solid rock of the Word.

Amos grasps Joseph's foot. "Father, Your Word is a promise to us, Your servants. You say, 'Rejoice in the Lord alway: and again I say, Rejoice. Let your moderation be known unto all men. The Lord is at hand. Be careful for nothing; but in every thing by prayer and supplication with thanksgiving let your requests be made known unto God. And the peace of God, which passeth all understanding, shall keep your hearts and minds through Christ Jesus'. We rejoice in You always and thank You for Joseph. Heavenly Father, we place Joseph at Your feet and ask for complete healing. He is Yours. Your will be done. In Jesus's name, Amen."

The pastor's shoulders tremble. "Show us Your power. Heal him. I beg You."

On a chair across the bed from her husband, Mary leans forward and rests her head on the blanket covering Joseph's chest.

Amos kneels beside Pastor Thatcher. Silence engulfs the room while the storm rages outside and within their hearts.

The pastor glances at Amos. "Go get a chair, Amos."

"Yes, preacher." Amos rises on creaking knees and halts. "Listen. The rain, the wind ... I don't hear anything."

Silence. A low rumble. Then a boom shakes everyone's world. And mine.

John and Mary jerk upward. The entire house quakes. The floorboards quiver beneath their feet. Windows rattle. Dishes tremble in the hutch. The iron poker next to the fireplace crashes onto the floor. Pastor Thatcher and Amos rush from the bedroom and into the living area. Amos whips open the front door. The Thatcher children scramble onto the front porch near their father while Mary remains with Joseph.

"Esther, I'm scared." Sarah wraps her arms around her big sister's waist. Esther strokes her sister's hair.

Everyone stares across the land. The horses stamp around in their stable. They bang against the wooden stall. The family's one cow bellows. The chickens squawk in the chicken coop. The coop door hits against the frame. A strong wind whips across the yard.

My limbs creak and strain against each other. My leaves plummet to the ground. Hail pellets the size of tiny pebbles hit the porch, steps, and yard.

"Look." John Michael picks up pellets.

"Ice." Sarah releases her grip around Esther and accepts the bits from John Michael.

"Don't eat it, Sarah," John Michael demands.

White pieces cover the yard. Moments later, the hailstorm stops.

Lightning streaks cross the sky in rapid succession. Thunder roars. "Something's about to happen." Pastor Thatcher frowns. Large rain drops thump the earth. The wind whips their clothes against their bodies. The pastor shouts, "Get inside."

Too late.

A sharp, jagged line of white races from the sky and strikes my largest limb. White fire blazes down my side. I groan as a crack begins at my top and descends. I split down the middle, two halves crashing onto the wet earth. The yard vibrates. Everyone runs into the house. Amos bolts the front door behind them.

"Whew." John Michael grins. "This storm's incredible."

Esther eyes widen. "The storm is frightening, and our big oak tree is ruined."

"The power of our God." Pastor Thatcher rakes a hand through his hair. "I'm grateful the oak did not fall on our house."

"Me too." Sarah grasps her father's hand.

Amos leans against the door. "Amen."

"M ... Mother ..." a slight, hoarse voice sounds from the other room.

Mary cries out, "John, come in here."

The pastor rushes into the bedroom with the others right behind him. He shoves the chair he had occupied earlier away from the bed. He stands over Joseph.

"Wa ... water." With slow momentum, Joseph pushes upward and the bed creaks. "Thirsty."

Mary's stares at her son. "Esther, get a glass of water." Her oldest daughter dashes from the room.

"A miracle." Amos beams.

"Son." The pastor leans over and hugs Joseph.

"Be careful, John." Mary's eyes gleam.

Pushing through the others, Esther hands the glass to her father, and he assists Joseph. After three swallows, Mary takes the glass, places the cup on the nightstand, and touches Joseph's forehead.

Mary's eyes widen. "He does not feel warm."

"Look." Pastor Thatcher grasps Joseph's face between calloused hands. "His eyes and skin do not look ... yellow any longer."

"Father." Joseph twists his head from side to side, and the pastor drops both hands.

Pastor Thatcher settles on the edge of the bed. "How do you feel?"

While a strong, steady rain hits the house roof, everyone watches Joseph.

"Thirsty ... and stiff." Joseph bends a leg and pushes up further onto the pillows.

"Is he healed, Father?" Sarah stands at the footboard with the others behind her.

"I ... I do not know." The pastor shrugs. "There does not appear to be any more fever. Are you cold, hot?"

"More water, please." Joseph throws the blanket aside. "Can I get up?"

"Hold on, young man." Mary hands Joseph the glass of water. "You stay put."

Joseph gulps the water. "Why? What's happened?"

"You've been in bed for two weeks," John Michael explains. "I don't know how Mother got you to drink anything."

"He was in and out of consciousness." Mary shakes her head.

"Huh?" Joseph hands the empty glass to Mary and sits straighter.

"Do you remember coming home from the meeting?" Pastor Thatcher asks.

"Some. I didn't feel good. We left because of the sickness."

"Yellow fever," John Michael says.

Mary lifts her eyebrows. "Any headache? Dizziness?"

Joseph looks at his mom and shakes his head. "My head doesn't hurt as bad as on the ride back home." He scans the room. "Can I get up? Please."

"Joseph, I believe you're healed." Amos pats the restored boy's foot. "Your father and mother have been at your side these past two weeks. Praying over you. Reading Scripture over you. Our congregation has been praying too."

"Thanks." Joseph examines the faces watching him. "I didn't mean to cause trouble."

"I'm thankful you're better." Mary dabs at her eyes with a handkerchief.

"We've been quarantined." John Michael glances at the others and back to his brother. "We couldn't leave the yard, and no one could visit."

"A miracle." The pastor stares at Joseph.

"When the rain stops, we'll send for Doc." Mary smiles. "If he thinks you're okay, you can get out of bed."

Grimacing, Joseph pushes back onto the pillow since Mother's words are final. "Father, what exploded?"

"What do you mean?"

"I heard an explosion and pounding in the yard." Joseph looks at the faces watching him.

Mary points downward. "The floor shook, and Joseph's eyes popped open."

"Father." Esther takes in a sharp breath. "When lightning struck the oak tree, was Joseph touched by God?"

Pastor Thatcher ponders her question. "Anything is

possible with God. An answer to my prayers." He gazes at Mary. "Our prayers."

"He does work in mysterious ways. Look at me with one arm."

Esther looks at Amos. "You're a hardworking man, Mr. Amos."

"Through God's power."

Joseph's stomach rumbles, and Sarah giggles.

"You hungry, little brother?" John Michael grins.

"You have an appetite?" Mary's eyes widen. "After all you've been through?"

"Yes. Please, I'd like something to eat." Joseph places a hand on his stomach.

"Come on, Sarah. We'll get food for him." Esther takes Sarah's hand and leads her out of the room.

"Nothing too rich. Bread or potatoes should be fine," Mary calls out after them.

"The storm has settled down." John Michael places an arm on the windowsill. "I'll go check on the animals."

"I'll go with him." Amos follows John Michael out of the room.

After kissing her son on the cheek, Mary reaches over the narrow bed, grabs her husband's hand and squeezes. "What a remarkable day."

Pastor Thatcher glances upward and mouths 'Thank You' while a tear slides down his cheek.

AN HOUR LATER, John Michael has gone to fetch the doctor. Mary, Esther, and Sarah visit with Joseph. Pastor Thatcher and Amos sit on the front porch. Near dusk, a slight breeze flows around the gentlemen, and lanterns from inside the house reflect light through the front windows onto the porch. A short distance away, I lay divided on the front yard.

Amos sways back and forth in a rocking chair staring at me. "You have a mess in your yard."

"My son is okay. Nothing else matters."

"Praise the Lord." Amos taps the chair arm with his fist.

"Praise the Lord, indeed." Pastor Thatcher stretches into the back of the rocking chair where he sits. "Thanks for coming over."

"I'm your friend."

"A great friend you are. I believe we have witnessed a miracle. These past two weeks have been horrible for Mary and me." The pastor glances at Amos and back at me. "I thought he would die. How could I doubt God?" He leans forward. "Does that make me unfaithful?"

"No, sir. Because God is always faithful to His Word."

"I was angry with God."

"At one time or another, I imagine all believers feel the same way. I did when I was lying in excruciating pain deciding if I would keep my arm and risk infection or have my arm chopped off. Remember, Doc made me decide. Cora would not chime in, said the decision was mine."

"I apologize, Amos. I was not—"

"No apologies. You were there for me. The visits and prayers you, your family, and our friends provided, helped me through one of the worst times of my life. The past two weeks have been about your son and your family's health." Amos smiles and grips the chair arm. "Still angry?"

"No." The pastor chuckles. "I want to shout what He did for us from the mountaintop."

"Then you should."

Pastor Thatcher considers Amos's words. "Sunday is right around the corner."

"God has handed you a sermon and a testimony with Joseph's sickness and healing. Go shout your message, preacher."

"I believe He has." Pastor Thatcher stands and leans a shoulder against the porch column. "The Lord opened my son's eyes and lifted him up. I had my doubts over the past two weeks, but God is wonderful. He pulled Joseph through the midst of the storm." He stares at me. "I wish ... this will sound crazy, but I want to mark today."

"An important day in your life. You have your son back." Amos stops rocking and leans forward. He points a finger toward me. "Sure is a shame. The tree had to be over a hundred years old."

"The branches are huge. The cleanup will be a bear."

"Oak is a hearty wood." Amos stands and props against the opposite column. "Preacher, the oak would make fine furniture."

The pastor straightens. "Yes. You and the men from the sawmill, could you make something to commemorate Joseph's healing?"

"We can. Any ideas?"

"Something we can share with everyone. A reminder of what God did. Maybe something for our country church."

"We should be able to get nice, long boards out of the tree."

The two men look at each other and say in unison, "A pew."

"That'll work." Amos grins. "I'll talk with a few men. I'm sure Mr. Charles will let us use the sawmill after hours."

"John Michael and I will help, and if Doc believes Joseph is able, he will too. Although, we do not work at the sawmill, I want our hands involved. I want Joseph to understand he was on death's doorstep, and now, he's a walking testimony for God."

"We'll honor what God has done this wonderful day." Amos slaps the preacher on the back.

Pastor Thatcher places an arm around Amos's shoulder. "We know who the giver and taker of life is. Today, God continued to bless me with my son here on earth. Let us give Him all the glory."

3

1865: AN ENCOUNTER WITH GENERAL SHERMAN

I have been pushed up against the wall of Pumpkin Creek United Church for months. Converted to a temporary Confederate hospital, dried blood stains mark the plank flooring and smear the once-white walls of the church. Dirtied sheets rest on a few pews, and I am thankful they are not on me. Pillows weigh down an unused cot stationed alongside the wall opposite my position. Two lit candles perch on the altar table, a half-used one on a small table, and another in the windowsill above me. Their dim light casts shadows along the walls.

Midway through the Civil War, and under the charge of Pastor John Thatcher, our church bustled with activity. Tents were erected in the churchyard because of the number of sick and wounded soldiers. Amos and several female citizens assisted at the hospital every day. Now, the church is more of a base where stragglers wander into camp or are dropped off by comrades. With few men around, women and children still congregate here and assist, hope for nourishment, or look for each other's company.

Despair hangs in the air and surrounds what should be a holy place. The war affects every person I see. Worn clothes hang on thin bodies. Hands and fingers bleed from hard work. In the darkness, whimpers sound from women and children left alone.

Amos rests on me and leans a weary head against the wall. After a few deep breaths, he pulls a silver timepiece from his left vest pocket. He holds the watch toward the candle's soft glow. Ten minutes before nine. The watch remains in his palm, and Amos looks toward the open door.

The floorboard creaks under the weight of Pastor Thatcher. With a gaunt face and thinning hair, the pastor's shoulders hunch over as though he bears the weight of the cross over his back. If time has not aged him, the war has.

"Not much longer." Amos sighs.

"Yes. Malcolm and the girls are settled. They're trying to sleep."

"I hope the rumors are true, and the war is about at an end."

"Me too. God-willing, an end is near. I pray for the sake of these women and children." Pastor Thatcher pulls a hand down over his face. "And us."

"The Confederacy is pushing toward the capitol. Do you believe Lee will surrender?"

With a creased brow, the pastor shrugs and sits on me. "I pray someone surrenders soon."

"Won't happen tonight, and we have to send Malcolm and his daughters on the boat heading for Roanoke Island." Amos places the watch in the vest pocket and lifts a small sack. "I have a little bread for them."

Malcolm and his two small daughters, Priscilla and Ella, wandered into camp after the destitution at the Greene Plantation had become too much for Mrs. Greene and her daughters to manage. Mrs. Greene and her remaining family left the plantation and headed north to stay with her cousin. The few freed slaves who had remained with her on the plantation departed on their own, seeking a new life. The Greene Plantation was the only home Malcolm, Priscilla, and Ella had known.

Malcolm had heard the pastor was a good man and would help anyone in need. Still afraid for their lives, the family hid in the woods at the first sound of voices. With small daughters, the journey was tedious. After two days, Malcolm and his daughters arrived on the church's doorstep needing food and water.

Amos frowns. "If they aren't on the boat by four in the morning, Pete will leave without them."

"I pray Roanoke Island is a safe haven for Malcolm and his girls."

"Me too." Amos scans the doorway. "We'll head out at midnight." Amos sucks in air and releases the deep breath. "I want to have plenty of time."

"That's a good idea." The pastor darts eyes toward the few candles in the church. "You want a lantern?"

"No. There's enough moonlight. We'll head due east until we reach the river and follow along the riverbank."

Before the war, Pumpkin Creek was a prosperous sawmill community. Those who did not work at the mill raised pigs, tended farms, or worked on the Greene Plantation. Amos oversaw the mill at the beginning of the war when wagons and carts were crucial for the Confederate Army, but the need stopped when Union forces gained more control of the area.

I am thankful Pastor Thatcher and Amos corralled our community of left-behind women and children to serve alongside them.

Pastor Thatcher leans his head back. "No word from Joseph or John Michael. Mary and I are sick with worry." He hesitates. "I pray they are alive and safe."

The Thatcher boys headed off to war, with John Michael

leaving behind a wife and one-year-old son. I long for the day when the pastor's sons walk through these church doors again.

"You're worried, my friend." Amos scrutinizes the pastor's face "And what do we do when we're worried?"

"Pray." Pastor Thatcher raises his head and places a hand on Amos's shoulder. The two men bow their heads. "Almighty God, we ask You to end the war and pull our country back together again. Our community has lost loved ones and friends. Bring my boys and our loved ones back home. We need Your strength, Lord. Bless the workers here and allow us to do Your will. Heal the wounded and the sick. Father, we ask—"

Outside, horse hooves thump the earth and halt. A woman shrieks. Quick, loud strides pound up the church's wooden steps and through the opened door. "Is there a physician here?"

Amos jerks up. "Federals."

Pastor Thatcher's body tenses. The war has pulled him in three directions—God's way, the Union way, and the Confederate way. As a pastor, his way is to lead his flock and others to salvation, not death. Each day the pastor kneels under the cross attached on the front wall and prays for God's direction, to do what is right in His eyes. He stands. "I am Pastor John Thatcher."

"General William T. Sherman," the man says.

Amos gasps. "How dare you enter our church?"

General Sherman remains silent. His presence commands attention.

"What do you want, General?" The pastor's eyes narrow.

"We are not here to cause any harm." The general glances over his shoulder. "Bring him in." Beyond the doorway, horses snort. A man grunts. His groans remind me of a human in pain. Within a minute, two soldiers enter with a Union soldier between them. General Sherman demands, "He needs quinine."

Pastor Thatcher rushes toward a cot in the corner topped with supplies. Amos is not quick to assist. "Amos, please." With hard eyes, Amos stands, walks over, and helps clear away the necessities. The pastor glances at the general. "Here. Put him here."

"Do you have any quinine?" Dressed in a blue uniform smudged with dirt, the general stands tall.

"No supplies in a long time." Amos stares at the general.

"Amos, let me," Pastor Thatcher pleads. "Please go check with Mary on the quinine."

"We do not have any." All eyes turn and focus on the preacher's wife walking into the church. The war has been hard on Mary. Thin, with white hair pulled into a sloppy knot at the back of her head, she continues, "I only have tea."

"Tea?" Questions the general. "Will the brew work?"

"I don't know. Folks have gotten better, others …" Mary pushes stray hairs off her face.

"Men, put him on the cot." The two soldiers obey the general.

"Amos, please get me rags and water." Mary glances around. "John, I need a small table, another candle, and a chair by the bed. I'll get the tea. You men, please get his coat off."

"Yes, ma'am." The general motions for the soldiers to remove the sick man's coat.

Several long minutes later, Mary bundles the man up in a sheet and blanket, lays a wet cloth on his forehead, and attempts spoon feeding him the tea. Sweat covers the man's feverish face.

Amos pulls the watch halfway from the vest pocket and checks the time again.

The general approaches Mary. "If no quinine, what's in the tea?"

"A concoction of bark from the dogwood and willow trees.

The brew will not work as fast as quinine, but the bark is all we have."

"Thank you, ma'am." With an index finger, the general touches his hat's brim.

The pastor returns with black coffee for the soldiers. Surprised, the soldiers look at the general. When he nods acceptance, they reach with eagerness for the cups.

"Thank you." Watching Amos, General Sherman accepts the coffee and motions for the soldiers to sit.

"Amos," the pastor points toward the door, "please go outside and check on the women and children.

"Please see our horses have water," the general orders.

Amos glares at him, turns, and walks out.

"General, let us take a seat. My wife will attend the sick man." Pastor Thatcher points at me.

I have heard talk of the man, the words harsh. The general's posture remains straight with eyes surveying the church's interior before he faces me. I suspect nothing gets past him. Deep lines run from the outer edges of General Sherman's nose down to the corners of a strong mouth. He looks formidable, and I am glad I do not have to fight against the Union army. When the general sits, a sword attached at his hip bumps against me with a dull thud.

General Sherman removes his hat, places the headpiece on me, and sips the coffee before pulling the kerchief away from his neck. "How do you folks survive the south's warm weather?"

The pastor sits beside him, savors a sip of coffee, and smirks. "We are used to the heat and humidity."

The general wipes his face with the cloth. "At a small farmhouse, a woman told us about this church hospital."

"Did you ... was the lady ... harmed?"

"No. I appreciated her help." The general looks at Mary. "I appreciate your assistance and your wife's."

"Why are you here, General? I would not expect such an interest in a soldier from you."

The general stares at the floor before answering, "I care about the welfare of all my men, and this soldier is the son of a friend. I promised I would do everything in my power to protect him."

"The father must be a dear friend."

"As the Proverb says, 'a friend who sticks closer than a brother.'"

Pastor Thatcher's eyebrows lift when he hears the Scripture from the war-worn general. A number of the Union's war tactics have been brutal. He rests the coffee cup on me. "Sir, you have attacked civilians and burned homes. I am not sure I believe you care for people's welfare."

With a stern face, the general acknowledges, "Yes, I have destroyed livelihoods. We are at war and will fight to the end." He pauses and tastes the coffee again. "I will not harm your camp or anyone here."

"Thank you."

Pastor Thatcher relaxes back against me and appears to take the general at his word. What else is possible? The preacher is not a soldier. Now, Amos could have been. "This war is ravaging our country. I do not know how much longer Mary and I are able to go on."

A groan sounds from the sick man, and the general watches him.

"I've lost several friends in the war," the pastor says.

"You have sons in the Confederacy?"

"Yes, sir." Pastor Thatcher glances at Mary, and she stifles a sob. "War is hard for us all. No word from our loved ones. I pray my boys come back home."

"I need more tea." Mary stands and departs from the church.

Amos appears at the door and motions for the pastor. "A moment."

The pastor joins him, and they speak in hushed tones. After a few moments, Amos turns and walks back into the night. The preacher returns to General Sherman.

"General, the North seeks to abolish slavery."

"Yes."

"We have three freed slaves outside who need to catch a boat headed for Roanoke Island."

"You are a sympathizer?" General Sherman arches an eyebrow. "Pastor, I do not know if you are playing with fire, as most men in the South would hang you if they found out, or if you are a man of deep faith."

"A man of deep faith. I have to do what is right."

"I understand slaves seek refuge on the island."

"Malcolm and his daughters need a new life. All they have known is a life of bondage."

General Sherman drains the coffee cup when Mary walks back inside with a steaming cup of tea. The sick man mutters garbled words while the other soldiers doze on a nearby pew.

"The reason why your friend is anxious?"

"Yes. I never owned slaves and neither did he. Since our church is near the river, folks have sought refuge with us until we get them on a boat. We move at night. Safer for all involved."

"You treat others with respect."

"I try." Pastor Thatcher glances at the Union soldiers and back to the general. "We are tired, General, as are your weary soldiers. We want the war over and our families back together."

"Freed slaves seek a new life on Roanoke Island, but they

do not understand. Life is hard, and disease flourishes on the crowded colony."

"I understand. Malcolm is a man and makes his own decisions. He thinks this is best. At midnight, Amos and I will lead them to the boat landing."

The general holds up a hand. "No. I will send a man. Is Amos trustworthy with my soldier?" The general cuts watchful eyes toward the door and back at the preacher.

"Yes. Although Amos will not like the idea, he will do what I ask."

"Good. After a rest, I will inform my soldiers."

A half hour before midnight, General Sherman approaches the soldiers. Pastor Thatcher speaks with Mary. Whispered conversation resonates through the dim church. When Amos reappears, the preacher informs him of the plan. Amos scowls, not too happy with the notion of a Union soldier for a companion, but at least, Malcolm and the girls will be on their way to freedom.

I watch in awe—two opposing sides join together to save a family. Oh, how God works in His ways to fulfill His plans.

Malcolm, Priscilla, Ella, Amos, Mary, and Pastor Thatcher huddle at the front of the church. General Sherman and the soldiers walk over and stand a couple of feet behind them. Pastor Thatcher prays.

"Dear Father in Heaven, place your hand upon Malcolm, Priscilla, and Ella. Surround them with Your hedge of protection as they make the journey to Roanoke Island. Give them the provisions needed. Give them good health. May they grow old and keep You in their hearts. Watch over Amos and his companion. Keep them safe. And Father, we beg of You to end the war and reunite our country as a God-fearing nation. In Jesus's name, amen."

"Amen." Amos's arm shoots upward.

"Thank you, Pastor," one soldier says, and the general nods in affirmation.

"Pastor Thatcher, y'all have been good to us. Thank you for all you did for us folks around here." Malcolm's eyes shine. "I will never forget you." Malcolm hugs the pastor, and Mary wraps her arms around the young girls. After saying their goodbyes, Amos, a Union soldier, Malcolm, Priscilla, and Ella leave the church.

Malcolm and his daughter's deserve freedom. God be with them.

NEAR DAYBREAK, Mary still nurses the sick soldier, and General Sherman stands across from her with a cup of coffee between his hands. "Will he survive, Mrs. Thatcher?"

"I'm hopeful. The fever is down." She places spoonful after spoonful of tea at the sick man's lips and pushes the liquid into his mouth. The soldier drops back against the pillow. Mary glances at the general who studies her. "Do you have children, General?"

"Yes, ma'am."

"End this war, for the sake of all our children."

The slightest smile touches General Sherman's mouth. "My wife asks the same of me."

She looks him in the eye. "If you men would listen to your wives, in all likelihood, our country would not be in such a mess."

"You may be correct, Mrs. Thatcher."

"Word is, you are a confident man ... and ruthless."

"Confident? Yes. Would my troops follow an unconfident man? No. War is hell, and the welfare of my men is of the utmost importance." He sighs. "They follow my orders."

"My husband takes orders from God," Mary says as Pastor Thatcher reenters the church.

"Mrs. Thatcher, I am not without my own losses." The general sits in the chair opposite her. "My six-month-old son died from pneumonia in December while I was away fighting a war. My wife, my children, and I are devastated."

Mary nods and returns her attention to the sick soldier.

The pastor stops behind Mary and places a hand on her shoulder. "We pray for you, General."

"For me, the enemy?"

"God's Word tells us to pray for the enemy."

"My wife, Eleanor, prays for me daily. She is a devout Catholic."

Remarkable how the notorious General Sherman interacts with a southern preacher and his wife. The general's reputation has been heralded throughout the South, but maybe, he is as tired of the war as everyone around here.

A tear slips down Mary's cheek. "I want my sons home again, General."

The general drains the coffee cup and stands. The remaining soldier approaches. "All is fine outside. Awaiting your orders, sir."

"He's too sick to ride," Mary says.

"Gen ... General." The sick man reaches out.

"Rest." Mary pushes the soldier's outstretched arm back down onto the bed.

The general looks at the man. "You get better. Sergeant Clark will return and escort you to our next destination. Your father and I want you well. I will see you soon."

The sick man attempts a smile, exhales, and drops back further into the musty pillow.

Pastor Thatcher says, "We will do our best for your man, General."

"I believe you. When they return, have the sergeant wait until he is able to ride again." The general glances at his friend's son before saying to the other soldier, "Prepare to leave."

"Yes, sir." The soldier looks at the pastor and Mary. "Thank you, sir. Ma'am." He exits the church.

Mary hands the general a small pouch from her apron pocket. "Here, the tea blend I made for him. In case you or someone else gets sick."

A crease forms between the general's brows. "Thank you. You did not have to—"

"I know. If my sons were ever in your company, I pray you would show them kindness." Mary turns her attention back to the patient.

The general and the pastor step over near me. General Sherman picks up the blue hat and places the cap on his head.

"General Sherman, while in my power, I will not let anything happen to your soldiers, and I will pray for all involved in the war, including you." Pastor Thatcher sticks out a hand toward the general. The military man shakes the pastor's hand and strides to the door.

The general pauses in the doorway and does not turn around. "Your sons' names?"

"John Michael and Joseph Everett Thatcher."

Sherman tilts his head in the direction of the sick man. "His father calls me Cump." The general steps over the threshold, descends the church steps, and disappears into the night.

I do believe General Sherman has extended a token of respect to Pastor Thatcher and Mary. If a man such as the general shares a nickname, he must hold them with high regard.

With raised brows, Pastor Thatcher looks at Mary. Her jaw drops.

By the end of summer 1865, our temporary hospital is no more. Women and children have headed back to their homes to rebuild their life, a number of wives without husbands and fathers to their children.

In the church, I am back in a normal spot for a pew and face forward. With a total of twelve pews, six on each side of the small aisle, I am the back pew on the left side. Years ago, when the plaque commemorating Joseph's healing was attached on the top, outer side of my right armrest, I realized my home would always be on the left side of the aisle which is fine by me. I want folks seeing what God did in Joseph's life.

Pastor Thatcher stands at the front behind the lectern and turns a page in his Bible. Mary and their daughters sit on a front row with Amos, Cora, and their three daughters on the opposite front pew. Women, children, and two men sit among the additional eleven pews situated in the church. When the church door opens, heads turn toward the interruption.

In walk two men wearing torn and dirty clothes. One has wavy hair that has seen better days, and the other sports a cap with longer hair pulled away from a scarred face. The older man's face is covered with a scruffy beard. The younger man's beard is short, and a red scar runs down from his temple to the cheekbone and toward the nose. Their clothes droop from scrawny bodies. Mary and her daughter-in-law, Elizabeth, stare at the intruders. After several seconds, recognition hits the women. They jump up from their seats. Mary and Elizabeth rush to the intruders and hug them. Pastor Thatcher hurries behind Mary.

"Joseph." Mary's voice quivers.

"John Michael?" Elizabeth's hands melt against her cheeks, and John Michael engulfs her in his arms.

The Thatcher's embrace each other, and friends circle around them. Cora pats Joseph on the back and wipes away tears. Amos points heavenward. Folks attempt asking questions of the Thatcher boys, and at the moment, hugs and tears abound too much for a reply. What a wonderful homecoming for the Thatcher family.

"Little John." Tears fill John Michael's eyes.

The now five-year-old boy hesitates.

"He's your pa." Elizabeth's face beams.

"Pa." Timid at first, Little John grasps John Michael's hand.

Overwhelmed, John Michael picks up Little John and holds the boy close as though he will never let his son go. Mary squeezes her way between her boys, hugging them and planting scattered kisses on their cheeks.

"God has answered another prayer," the pastor chokes out. He hugs Joseph.

"A long journey, Father." Joseph grins. "I'm glad we're home."

"But how? Where were you?" The pastor looks at each son.

John Michael places his son down next to him. The crowd listens. "We ended up in a Union prison, Camp Chase in Ohio."

"We were together throughout the entire war," Joseph says.

"God had His hand on us for sure," John Michael glances at his brother before continuing, "although we are skinnier, we didn't starve or get sick as a horde of those around us did. We followed in your footsteps, Father. We never lost our Bibles." From worn trousers, John Michael pulls a small, crinkled book while Joseph removes one from a shoulder sack.

Joseph smiles. "The Federals didn't confiscate them either."

"We prayed with the men. Read Scripture. Men were saved." John Michael hands the small Bible to Little John.

The pastor grasps each son's shoulder. "Thank You, Lord."

With fingertips, Elizabeth dabs at her eyes. "When did they release you?"

"One day back in April," John Michael says, "a colonel entered the barracks and called both our names. We thought he was going to shoot us. During the war, prisoners were called out and never seen again. We followed the colonel, and he handed us a piece of paper."

Joseph picks up the story. "For our release. Not a hair on our head was to be touched by any Union soldier. The colonel said if we didn't arrive home, the fault was ours not the Union Army. The soldiers opened the gates, and we never looked back." Joseph reaches into the shoulder sack and hands a folded, worn piece of paper to his father. "The colonel gave us this."

Pastor Thatcher opens the paper and reads.

"By order of General William T. Sherman.

John Michael Thatcher and Joseph Everett Thatcher of the Confederate Army are hereby released from any and all Union Army prisons. No harm is to be done to these two men by any member of the Union Army. If any soldier disobeys my order, he will be hanged."

"Signed, General William T. Sherman, and under his name, he wrote,"... The pastor meets Mary's gaze ... "Cump."

4

1882: A MAN AFTER GOD'S OWN HEART

The congregation finishes the well-known song Amos had loved singing, "My Hope is Built on Nothing Less."

Pastor John Michael glances over at Elizabeth, the pianist, and smiles before he looks back to those who have gathered for Amos's memorial service. He lowers middle-aged hands indicating the congregation should be seated. "A wonderful song. One of Amos's favorite hymns. I imagine Amos is up there singing and praising the Lord. If he could see us, I don't imagine he would want any tears or unhappiness."

Amos's widow, Cora, her three daughters, and their husbands, fill the first pew on the right side of the sanctuary. Her eleven grandchildren sit on the pew behind them. She and her daughters blot tears from their eyes.

"Amen." Retired, sixty-five-year-old Pastor John Everett Thatcher agrees with his oldest son's words.

After the war, John Michael answered the calling to become a pastor. Pastor Thatcher mentored John Michael the best he could and encouraged him to attend seminary. When

John Michael attended college, Elizabeth and Little John lived with Pastor Thatcher and Mary. Elizabeth worked as a seamstress in town supplementing their income. Upon John Michael's return home, the elder Pastor Thatcher stepped down, and John Michael accepted the pastoral position at Pumpkin Creek United Church. Little John, a twenty-two-year-old man, oversees the crops on the Greene Plantation that Obadiah Ward, a business man from Raleigh, North Carolina, purchased and rebuilt.

Pastor John Michael places a hand on the Bible that rests on the lectern. "A month ago, when Amos went to be with our Lord and Savior, Cora wanted a small graveside burial."

"That's all he wanted," Cora says.

"He was a humble man, Mrs. Cora. We loved him with all our heart. Thank you for allowing us to honor Amos's memory today." John Michael glances over the crowded twenty-four pews. "Thank you all for being here. I'm happy to see my sisters and their families, folks from the sawmill where Amos spent most of his time, and visitors in attendance."

Since Amos was a man who served God and others, I am not surprised at all the folks in attendance paying their respects to the Wilson family. Thank the good Lord the members expanded the building.

After the war, poverty and devastation surrounded us. With Reconstruction, the sawmill reopened providing much needed jobs in our area. With more people, more room was required in our church. The renovation was long but worth the wait.

During the expansion, I, along with all the other pews, were pushed together and covered with sheets. I did not enjoy the concealment but understand protection was needed. The small renovation increased the sanctuary's size with enough room for twelve pews on each side of the center aisle. The area where the pastor's lectern stands was raised the height of two steps with the piano resting several feet away from the lectern. The altar table sits at the end of the center aisle and in front of the podium. Offering plates and a candelabra rest on top of the table. In addition, the folks built an outdoor shelter for picnics and social gatherings.

My time in the church during the renovation was short because more pews were needed. Since Joseph Thatcher apprenticed at the sawmill with Amos, the two used their talents for the Lord and built the pews. While the other pews remained behind, I rode in the back of a wagon to the sawmill where Joseph and Amos took my measurements and created more identical pews. I relished seeing green grass, spring flowers, and trees in full bloom. Oh, how I miss the experience of spring, summer, winter, and autumn. In due time, all the pews were removed from the church, sanded down to our original wood, and stained a medium brown color. Several pews have plaques attached, similar to mine, with members' names or a name in memory of someone etched on a small, gold plaque. I disliked the chaos of construction work. However, the result was worth my discomfort. At present, I reside on the left side of the sanctuary, the sixth pew from the front.

Each time Joseph enters the church, he walks by and ensures no smudges are on my plaque. I am glad I adopted his middle name. I appreciate what Joseph represents—a godly, upright family man. Plus, God struck me with lightning and healed Joseph at the same time. That was no accident. God knew what He was doing. So, taking Everett as my name seemed right.

"Now," Pastor John Michael motions for Cora, "Cora will play the piano, and her daughters will sing "Amazing Grace" in honor of their father."

Cora takes her place at the piano, and her three daughters

stand behind the lectern. Their voices are strong, yet soft as they sing. I see their mother's pride flashing in her eyes while they hold their composure through all the verses. The crowd claps after they finish and step down.

Pastor John Michael looks at the first row and finds Joseph. "My brother will say a few words."

At forty-years-old, strong, and in good physical shape, Joseph strides to the front. No one would believe this is the same Joseph whose mother worried over him as a child.

Without thinking, Joseph touches the scar on the side of his face which will always be a reminder of time spent in the Union prison. "Mr. Amos was a hard-working man who instilled a strong work ethic in me." Joseph looks at his parents sitting on the front row opposite the Wilson's. "Father and Mother, you taught me to work hard too. When I returned from the war, I felt lost. I didn't feel called to become a minister as John Michael did."

The elder pastor sends an encouraging smile toward Joseph.

"God showed me my talents, and one is a love for woodworking. Mr. Amos noticed and discussed my gift with Father. He took me under his wing and taught me the basics of woodworking, the different types of wood, and their uses. Mr. Amos allowed me creativity in the work, and if I made a mistake on a project, he insisted I begin again and do the job right." Joseph's eyes shine when he turns toward Mrs. Cora, his mother-in-law.

With her crumpled handkerchief, Cora dabs at her eyes.

"Mr. Amos recommended me as foreman at the sawmill. He was a mentor and a man of strong character, a second father if you will." Joseph pauses and swallows. "I will miss him." Joseph steps down and takes a seat beside Kay, his wife.

Kay, what a beautiful, godly woman. Amos played matchmaker in bringing his daughter and Joseph together. From the conversations I have overheard, Amos took the initiative and invited Joseph over for dinner at the Wilson home on more than one occasion. Soon, a courtship began between Joseph and Amos's youngest daughter. Within two years after the war, Kay became Joseph's bride.

"Kind words, brother." John Michael steps back up, stands at the lectern, and gazes at two women. "We have two special guests who have kept in contact with Mother, Father, and Mrs. Cora over the years." Two ladies walk forward and stop next to him. "These are Priscilla and Ella." John Michael whispers a few words to Priscilla, who smiles.

"Thank you, Pastor Thatcher, Pastor John Michael, and Mrs. Cora for letting us speak." Priscilla glances toward the older pastor before focusing on the congregation. "Pumpkin Creek United Church holds a special place with us. When Ella was six and I was seven, we left the Greene Plantation with our father, Malcolm. With no one working the fields, no money, no food, and a home falling apart, Mrs. Greene left the plantation with her daughters. She encouraged Father to head north where he'd have more opportunity as a freed man. We were scared, but Father demanded we keep moving and find this church."

Ella steps closer to the lectern. "He'd heard the pastor helped folks, all folks. Situated near the river, the church allowed a place of rest before our journey."

"I remember the night." The senior Pastor Thatcher's eyebrows lift. "Amos wasn't too happy with our visitor."

"Oh yes. General Sherman," Mary says. "A night I will never forget."

"I remember the men in uniforms." Ella frowns. "I didn't want to leave and walk through the woods in the dark. I felt safe here."

Priscilla points at the altar table. "Pastor Thatcher and Mr.

Amos prayed with us up near the front here while those soldiers stood nearby. I was scared. One of the Union soldiers escorted us to the boat. Mr. Amos led the way. Father carried Ella, and the soldier carried me. The soldier encouraged me and said the war would be over soon."

"I cried when we left the only home I had ever known." Ella wipes a tear from the corner of her eye. "I didn't understand where we were going or if anyone followed us. Mr. Amos stopped by a group of trees and whispered to me. He had helped others before us. He said he would die before he let anyone harm me or Priscilla." She looks at Cora. "One of the bravest men I have ever met."

"Yes, he was," Cora agrees.

"Mr. Amos made sure we were settled on the boat." Priscilla places a hand over her heart. "He gave us a small sack of bread and hugged us goodbye. He said he would wait until the boat left before he headed back to the church. Father assured him we would be fine. He didn't want Mr. Amos put out any more than he already had been."

Ella smiles at the Wilson family. "I peeked from a small window several times. Mr. Amos sat on the riverbank with a stick in hand, and the soldier remained out of sight among the bushes and trees."

Priscilla snivels. "Thank you all for helping us. The journey wasn't easy, but Father was determined. After we arrived on Roanoke Island, filth and sickness lived amongst us. Once Father realized the conditions were not good, he made another plan."

"From being there," Ella glances over the crowd, "I knew I wanted to help people. We left the island and reached Chicago. Once I finished school, I became a nurse, and Priscilla became a school teacher."

"Praise the Lord." Pastor John Michael tilts his head heavenward.

Priscilla shares how Mr. Jones, a tailor by trade, gave Malcolm a job and taught her father everything he knew about the tailoring business. Mrs. Jones enrolled Priscilla and Ella into school. On behalf of their father, the girls wrote to Pastor Thatcher, Mary, and Amos. Malcolm passed two years ago before his fiftieth birthday.

"Priscilla," Cora says. "Please share what your father did in honor of Amos."

"Yes, ma'am. While a slave, Father was known as Malcolm Greene. He wanted a name of his choosing, not the name of someone who owned him. Since Pastor Thatcher and Mr. Amos put their lives in danger by helping others, Father said these two men showed him respect, to remember what they did for us because, one day, we might have to make a difficult decision to do what is right even if we have to put our lives in danger."

Ella grasps Priscilla's hand. "Our father taught us to do what is right in God's eyes, as these two men did. Father had us write to Mr. Amos and ask permission before he moved forward." The sisters look at each other, and Ella continues, "For our surname, Father chose Wilson. Our father became Malcolm Wilson."

A man in the congregation says, "What a wonderful way to pay homage to Amos." Others in the sanctuary murmur their agreement.

"Thank you." Priscilla focuses on Cora. "When we heard about Mr. Amos's death, we knew we had to come pay our respects. If not for his courage, we might not have succeeded in finding our way to Roanoke Island." Priscilla looks at the pastor who helped her years ago. "Thank you for showing our father respect." She finishes, nods at Pastor John Michael, and the sisters move a step away from the lectern.

"Father, please come on up." Pastor John Michael motions, and the elder pastor moseys to the podium where he hugs Malcolm's daughters.

"Thank you for making the train ride down here. Mary and I are proud of you both—Priscilla, using your gift of teaching, and you, Ella, nursing. God led Malcolm and his family where He wanted you."

"Yes, He did," Priscilla says before she and Ella return to their seats.

The senior Pastor Thatcher steps behind the lectern and grasps the edges the same way he did when delivering a sermon. "I will miss my dear friend, Amos. I walk over here every day and spend time alone with the Lord. Before he passed, Amos would drop by and we'd chat or find something to do around here ... repairs, pulling weeds, or cleaning the windows."

"He considered you a brother, John." Cora smiles at the pastor.

"The feeling was mutual. After the funeral a few weeks ago, I wandered over to Amos's grave and talked with him. Oh, I know he's not there. He's with Jesus. Amos was a friend like the Bible speaks of. 'Greater love hath no man than this, that a man lay down his life for his friends.' This was Amos."

"He put his life at risk for our family. We are grateful." Priscilla reiterates from her seat.

"For you all and countless others." The older pastor glances over the congregation. "When Amos lost his arm, I thought he would die."

"Me too," Doc, gray-headed and retired, speaks up. "He made the right decision and had the arm removed."

"Amos asked me and Cora what he should do about the

arm. Keep what was sure to become infected or have Doc cut his arm off. He agonized through the pain questioning how he would support Cora and the girls. As Cora and I know, Amos was not a patient man."

"Amen." Cora raises a hand heavenward. Many folks chuckle.

"God taught him patience in His time. With one arm, Amos moved slower, dressed slower, did chores slower, and complained about the length of time jobs took at the sawmill."

"And the good Lord knows," Cora shakes her head, "he would not accept help from anyone. My Amos, a stubborn man at times."

Her daughters murmur their agreement, and others in the congregation do the same.

"God helped him and us through his painful season of life," Pastor Thatcher says. "The loss made him a better man. About a year after the accident, he told me he learned to lean on God more, read the Bible more, and pray more." The pastor glances toward Cora and her daughters. "Our one-armed friend, your husband and your father, touched more lives with one arm than most people do with two."

Snivels sound in the church from men, women, and children.

"And I believe as Amos stood before Christ, He said, 'Well done, good and faithful servant.'" Pastor Thatcher clears his throat. "Those are the words I want to hear. Those are the words we should all want our Lord to say to us." He pauses, bows his head, and those in the congregation do the same. "Dear Father in heaven, thank You for the life of Amos Wilson. Thank You for his friendship and the love he showered on family and friends. As we move forward without him on earth, please give Cora and her daughters Your strength with each passing day. We ask they recall precious memories of Amos and share them with their children. Let his legacy live on in generations to come. Surround us with Your comfort and peace. And Lord, if there is anyone here who does not believe in the saving grace of Jesus, I ask You to open their hearts and minds to receiving Christ as their Savior. To You, God, all glory be given. In Jesus's name. Amen."

"Amens" resound throughout the church.

Amos left behind a legacy of love and friendship to all who knew him. He was an upright man who served the Lord with honesty and integrity. With one arm, Amos worked hard, provided for his wife and daughters, and served Christ in the Pumpkin Creek community. His unnoticed deeds kept the church from falling into disarray. He prayed for and advised others when asked, and shared the truth with folks when they needed candidness. Amos pursued what was right in God's eyes. He was a man after God's own heart.

I will miss him.

5

1899: TIMES ARE CHANGIN'

I sit outside and watch the events happening around me.

A gentle breeze blows through the two dogwood trees in full bloom on the church property. Under the pavilion, ladies place fried chicken, ham, biscuits, green beans, potatoes, cakes, and pies on a long table. A few of the elderly sit at smaller tables and converse. On the church lawn, others stand and chat waiting on the preacher who will say a few words before the crowd eats. A man cooks popcorn in a large kettle over an open fire. Children and teenagers stand by watching the kernels pop. Near the outdoor shelter, a family prepares a puppet show. Two little girls admire the doll faces. Pumpkin Creek United Church members and visitors are in joyful spirits because today is a day of celebration.

The late nineteenth century brought changes and prosperity to the area. Our rural community continues as a farmer's paradise in the cotton and tobacco industries. The cotton mill built near the edge of town by the river brought in more jobs, and the railroad expanded across the state. Nowadays more folks travel into the area with newcomers settling on a more permanent basis which increased our membership and filled our pews to capacity on most Sundays. The pastor and elders discussed the prospect of a new church building, and the members agreed.

The Ward family—who had invested in the railroad sometime back and increased their wealth—were gracious enough to purchase the surrounding land where the smaller Pumpkin Creek United Church sat. They donated the property in order to build a bigger church.

During the long process of building the new church, my fellow pews and I remained in the old church, serving as we always had, waiting until the day we would be moved to our new location. Today, all the pews sit on the church grounds in neat rows because two days ago, the newly, stained floors were still tacky. Mrs. Johnston, Pastor Jeremiah Johnston's wife, suggested the pews be placed in the churchyard with the Sunday service held outside, and afterward, the men could transfer the furniture into the new sanctuary.

I appreciate the suggestion because I have always enjoyed a warm, spring day.

"Gather around, folks. I want to say a few words." Pastor Johnston, a middle-age man with a dark beard and dressed in a black suit, stands on a picnic table bench. "Pumpkin Creek United Church has been blessed over the years, and God continues to bless us. We've had much growth." He points at the new church building, and the crowd claps.

Besides the renovation, Pumpkin Creek United Church has had many changes. In 1884, Pastor John Michael and Elizabeth were needed back home in western North Carolina to care for Elizabeth's mother when she became ill. Little John and his new wife followed his parents. The word around the church was Little John secured a job in the building of George

Vanderbilt's mansion back in 1889. I had never heard of the Vanderbilt's, but the ladies of the church seemed impressed by the name.

From 1884 until 1885, traveling preachers filled the gap while the elders conducted a search for a new pastor. Each denomination has their own group of traveling preachers. These pastors go from church to church and assist for as long as needed when a congregation is without a preacher. The Reverend Claude Wentworth graced us with his presence from 1885 through the winter of 1893, before heading back to Charleston, South Carolina, where his extended family lived. Before securing Pastor Jeremiah Johnston in 1895, traveling preachers again filled in for the weekly services. One young, traveling preacher surprised me and the members when he arrived with two wives. The elders sent him and both wives packing. They never spoke of the 'preacher' again. Thus far, Pastor Johnston is a man built on biblical doctrine. I predict he will remain at the church for a number of years.

"First, thank God for what He has given us here at Pumpkin Creek." Preacher Johnston points a finger toward the sky before he continues. "Quite a few of us have lived through hard times and experienced the war, sickness, loss of loved ones and hunger, but our God has provided, and He is working through our church in this community."

"Yes, He is," fifty-seven-year-old Joseph Thatcher says. I remember the day when I was built to commemorate Joseph's healing. I cannot believe he has grandchildren.

Although Joseph and Kay's three daughters had moved away from the area in recent years, all six of their children are in attendance today. Pastor John Everett Thatcher, Mary Thatcher, and Cora Wilson have all gone to their heavenly home. Though God has blessed us with new faces in our congregation, I have a long history with the Thatchers, and I hope to always have their descendants at our church because they hold a special place in my heart.

The preacher finds Obadiah Ward and his grown son, Benjamin. "Thank you to the Ward family for donating the land for our new church and all you provide in our community and town." After Benjamin graduated from the University of North Carolina's School of Law, he came back to eastern North Carolina and practices law. Obadiah and Benjamin bought the sawmill where Joseph's sons, Amos and Paul, work.

"We have all been blessed," Joseph says, and others in the crowd murmur in agreement.

"Edward Thatcher." The preacher gestures, and the man steps forward. "Will be our new headmaster and teacher. Most of you remember, Edward's grandfather, John Everett Thatcher and his uncle, John Michael, served as pastors here before me. We all know his father, Joseph." Pastor Johnston scans the crowd. "We'll use the old church for our school building. A great number of families wanted an education for their children, so we're breaking the class size down by age group. Fourth grade and under will meet in the morning. Fifth through eighth will meet in the afternoon."

Edward touches the wire-rimmed glasses on his face. "Since I have talked with most families in our community, I will also use the afternoon session and assist those students seeking a higher education in preparation for college entrance." Edward grins. "Who knows, we could have a future doctor among us." Smiling and nodding, several folks look around at the school-age children and teenagers in the crowd.

The preacher glances toward a young woman who arrived last week. "Miss Laura White will be our lower-school teacher." When the crowd turns their attention her way, Laura smiles and offers a slight wave.

"Again, we are blessed to have these two teachers among

us." The pastor smacks his beard-covered lips together and chuckles. "We'd better get to the food before the fried chicken gets too cold. I will give thanks for our food. Let us bow our heads."

After Pastor Johnston finishes the prayer, Obadiah adds, "Young chaps, eat up. You'll need your strength this afternoon when you all move those pews." He chortles, a group of teenaged boys groan, and the crowd disperses among the church yard.

I am anxious to get inside the longer, wider, and bigger church building with more room for pews than our original one-room church. The building sits high off the ground on a brick foundation with six brick stairs leading to double front doors painted brown. The exterior of the church is painted white with four large windows on the side facing me, each window with eight panes of glass. Atop the pitched roof that slopes downward on both sides from the center ridge sits a decorative steeple with a slender spire protruding upward. A brick base supports the wooden sign near the dirt road inscribed with the following:

Pumpkin Creek United Church
Sunday Worship: 10:00 a.m.
Wednesday Prayer Meeting: 6:00 p.m.
Reverend Jeremiah Johnston

LATER IN THE AFTERNOON, the women clean the picnic tables and pack their belongings. The men begin the chore of moving the furniture into the church.

"Let us take two pews and place them on the podium," the

preacher directs and points at more men. "You all bring in the piano next."

"Yes, sir," a young man responds.

Sarah Ward places her hand on a pew back. "Joseph, you all did a wonderful job matching the new pews to our original ones."

"My boys, Amos and Paul, did most of the work," Joseph says. "I spend a few hours a day at the mill now. My age has slowed me down, and I enjoy spending more time with my grandchildren."

Sarah watches the men pick up and move furniture into the church. "Be careful with the pulpit. Looks heavy."

A man grunts as he lifts. "This piece is bigger than my bed headboard."

Laura touches the armrest of a pew. "These nameplates are a nice touch on the pews."

"Here's yours, Father." Edward points at me. His wife, Rebecca, shifts their newborn son, James, in her arms.

"I remember." Joseph nods. "Father and Mother thought I was going to die."

"We have heard the story too many times to count." Edward glances toward Laura. "Grandfather Thatcher was the pastor here. He, Father, and Uncle John Michael went to a Baptist meeting where Father contracted yellow fever."

"I was sick for two weeks," Joseph says.

Laura's eyes widen. "You survived. What a miracle."

Joseph recounts the events of the night he was healed.

"Father wanted to commemorate the night." Joseph points at my shining plate. "The pew is made from that fallen oak tree."

Laura rubs her hand along my seatback. "What a wonderful legacy. Something your grandchildren and great-grandchildren will remember."

"Excuse me, folks," the oldest of four men says, and those remembering me step away. The men, two on each end, bend and grasp me. After two years of waiting, I am on my way to my new position in the church.

The men struggle with me when they lift my oak frame higher and walk up the church steps, their breathing heavy. The double doors stand open, and we enter my new home. Once over the threshold, the men set me down to catch their breath.

Oh, my. The foyer is wide enough to hold four pews. The door to the preacher's study is on the left, and the broom closet is on the right. Several hooks protrude from the wall next to the closet, and a double-sized doorframe leads into the sanctuary.

Unbelievable. The sanctuary is huge with pews on either side of the center aisle.

"Left side." The oldest man grunts. The men set me down on the left side, eleventh row from the front of the church. "Hold on. Straighten your end." The man indicates with a finger. "That's good." The floor creaks a smidgen under the feet of the men when they head back out for more furniture.

Sunlight filters through the windows of my new home. The walls are white and a sharp contrast to the dark, stained floors and pews. Three steps lead up to the podium. I suspect the two pews placed behind the pulpit will be used for the choir members. The piano sits on the left side of the podium and an organ on the right. Today marks the first time Pumpkin Creek United Church has ever had an organ. Mrs. Sarah Ward said every church needs an organ, so she made the purchase and donated the instrument. I also heard she can play the organ. I cannot wait to hear the notes sound throughout our new church.

Sarah and Laura enter the sanctuary. Laura turns around

and surveys the new church. "My goodness. Your church is big."

"Yes, we will have forty pews in here, twenty on each side." Sarah scans the church interior. "God is good, and He is working in our community."

"Yes, He is." Laura places her hands on her hips. "I see your need for a school outside the city limits. I am excited to get started with my new position." She points upward. "Those three brass chandeliers are beautiful."

Sarah walks over near a back wall and touches a handle. "When the lever turns, the result is the chandeliers lower, and we light the candles."

"Amazing."

"Times are changing," Sarah, a woman ahead of her time, says. "A man, Thomas Edison, has invented something called electricity which will make the necessity for candles and lanterns obsolete." Sarah returns and stands by Laura. "I look forward to the convenience reaching our rural area."

"I have read about him and the cities where electricity is used."

"Our original church was one-room and used as a hospital during the War Between the States." Sarah spreads her hands. "Look at how far we have come. The world is changing according to God's plan. Have you seen the horseless carriages?"

With eyes wide, Laura gasps. "I have seen one. They are unbelievable."

The horseless carriage is all the boys and men talk about nowadays. I have overheard a couple of young men mention that when the price is more affordable, they hope to purchase this machine with wheels. Not a family who boasts about their riches, I suspect Sarah will have a horseless carriage soon enough.

"Anything is possible with God. One day, humans will travel in the air."

"Like a bird?" Laura wrinkles her nose. "Oh, Mrs. Ward, that's silly talk."

"God knows what the turn of the century will bring, dear. Only God knows."

Mrs. Sarah Ward is right.

God's plan in God's time. I once was a tree, now I am a pew, and I have been blessed to live in two homes called Pumpkin Creek United Church.

6

1908: BECOMING MRS. THATCHER

On this glorious Saturday afternoon in October, the sun shines and the leaves on the oak and maple trees are bright yellow and orange—the nicest month in eastern North Carolina and a great day for a wedding.

With the couple's family and friends crowded into the sanctuary, the ladies who assisted with the wedding preparations suggested leaving the door and windows open so the autumn breeze could flow inside. Good idea. Although, North Carolina has tons of creepy, crawly insects. The bugs will bother humans before they disturb me unless, the pests are termites. I despise termites because they will invade oak trees, which I was in my previous life.

Mr. White stands beside his daughter, Laura, the radiant bride. He gazes at her. "It is time."

Since so many are in attendance, my view is somewhat obstructed, but I can still hear everything. The doors leading from the vestibule into the sanctuary remain open with the bride and wedding party standing under the double entrance and near the back four pews. Folks in front of me and behind peer over their shoulders for a peek at the bride. Edward Thatcher stands at the front gazing at his bride with love-filled eyes. Everyone awaits her walk down the aisle.

"Wait," four-year-old Martha cries. "I forgot my teddy bear."

"Where is he?" Laura asks her soon-to-be stepdaughter.

Martha's seven-year-old brother, Luke says, "She left the bear in the buggy."

Edward glances at the pastor, and both men smile facing Laura and Martha.

"I need him." Martha pouts. "I put on the little black wedding suit you made for him."

Even though the wedding is about to begin, Laura knows how important the bear is to Martha. The stuffed bear was a gift from Suzanne Ward. With no children of her own yet, Suzanne indulges the youngsters in the church. The inventor of the teddy bear named the toy after President Theodore "Teddy" Roosevelt. I hear the bear has become a popular toy among children.

Laura looks at Luke. "Please go see if her bear is in the buggy." Luke drops the wedding train and runs outside.

Mr. White announces to the pastor, "Just a moment, please. We forgot something." He blushes and looks at the floor. Laura pats her father's arm. She is accustomed to the commotions and shenanigans of children since she lives life every day as a teacher.

With the pulpit removed for the ceremony, Pastor Jeremiah Johnston, his beard covered in gray, stands at the front and faces those in attendance. To the right of the preacher, Edward stands, waiting. Beside Edward, his nine-year-old son, James, shifts from foot to foot. Whispers resound among the people waiting for the ceremony to begin. Behind the preacher and off to the side, three candles stand in a tall iron candleholder. The two on the outer edges are lit. Once married, the couple will light the middle unity candle. The wedding decorations include greenery with yellow flowers, colorful against the sanctuary's white walls.

Laura and Edward have worked together educating the youth in the area. At the turn of the century, the county administration built a new school in the Pumpkin Creek community. Edward serves as the principal while Laura continues as a first-grade teacher. After Edward's wife passed, folks watched as the bond between the two grew.

Mrs. Sarah Ward was correct about changes coming to our community. Obadiah Ward was the first in our congregation to purchase a horseless carriage, and now, I hear more and more talk of a man named Henry Ford. Sarah had indoor plumbing installed in the Greene Plantation. Two brothers, Orville and Wilbur Wright, invented flying machines in Ohio and flew them in nearby Kitty Hawk, North Carolina. Thomas Edison's electricity lights up towns and cities and is predicted to spread out in the rural communities. Folks will now talk to each other from different locations through a device called a telephone. Sometimes, I cannot wait for the members arrival at the church where I learn of all the happenings in the outside world. Folks say progress is a wonderful thing, although I wonder if pews will lose their purpose and be replaced with something else.

Luke rushes in, reaches around the bride, and hands the bear to Martha. Laura smiles down at him and winks at Martha.

"Are we ready?" Mr. White asks.

Laura says, "Martha, do you remember what you are supposed to do?"

Holding the bear in one arm and her small basket of yellow rose petals with the other, Martha begins the procession down the aisle before the pianist strikes a key.

Pastor Johnston darts his eyes toward the pianist, and she taps the keys.

Dressed in a frilly, yellow dress, Martha steps with great care, one foot in front of the other until she is about one-third of the way. She glances back at Laura, eyes wide. "I forgot to throw them out."

She sits the basket down, takes out a handful of rose petals with her free hand, dashes back down the aisle, and tosses the petals onto the wooden floor. The folks sitting near the back of the church chuckle. Martha turns and walks back down the aisle. She picks up the basket, takes two tiny steps, puts the basket back down on the floor, removes a rose petal, and places the small spear on the floor. Edward motions for her to hurry.

She frowns. "I have to put the petals on the floor first."

Folks smile and grin at Martha while she does her job. At the end of my eleventh row, left side position, she leans in toward Mr. and Mrs. Obadiah Ward.

"Take one." Martha holds the basket toward him.

Obadiah picks out a rose petal. "Thank you, Sweet Pea."

Little by little, Martha continues down the aisle, stopping, placing her basket on the floor, taking out one petal at a time, and dropping pieces until she approaches the second pew from the front where her Grandpa Joseph sits. She stops and hugs him before Grandma Kay points toward the front. Martha continues onward.

"Good grief." James exclaims. He waves for Martha to hurry along.

With a loving expression on her face, Laura watches the little girl who will become her daughter in a few moments.

At last, Martha stops in front of Preacher Johnston and peers into her basket before dumping the remaining petals at his feet. The preacher chortles. With great finesse, she is finished with her job.

Martha's birth was a miracle. Edward's wife had a difficult pregnancy with her and passed away moments after Martha's birth, leaving Edward with a newborn and two small boys. The first year was difficult for him. Grandma Kay and Grandpa Joseph cared for his children while Edward continued working. Laura helped on Saturdays and Sundays, taking the boys on a picnic or into town to give Edward a break. Soon, Edward attended the picnics Laura planned for the children.

At Sarah Ward's nudging, Edward asked Laura if he could court her. Folks thought Laura would be an "ole maid" as she is one year shy of thirty. However, God had another plan for her.

With a huge grin on her face, Martha holds out the empty basket, and her father accepts the offering before placing the basket next to him on the floor. James places an arm around Martha's shoulders and pulls her over where she will stand beside him.

The preacher nods at the pianist, and she switches to the "Wedding March." The crowd watches the bride and her father walk down the aisle.

"Oh my," a woman gasps.

"She's beautiful," the lady next to her says.

The bride wears a long, ivory wedding dress covered in delicate lace. Her slenderness is emphasized by the fitted bodice, two-inch waistband, and flowing skirt. The train of the dress extends five feet in back of the garment, and with each step, the fabric whooshes against the floor. A high neckline accentuates Laura's delicate face, and her bright, blue eyes sparkle with joy.

Edward beams from ear to ear. He is a blessed man. Laura will make a wonderful wife and mother. Folks speak of her kindness and patience toward others which is all I have ever seen her demonstrate with regard to our members, youngsters in the church, and visitors.

Halfway down the aisle near me, Luke drops the train and stumbles on the material. The delicate fabric rips.

"Oh." Laura stops with a jerk and twists. Her father staggers to a stop.

"Uh-oh." Luke jumps back. "I'm sorry."

The music stops. Mr. White's jaw drops. Ladies cover their mouths with gloved hands.

"Oh, my goodness." A teenaged girl nearby stares at the torn dress and rumblings sound throughout the church.

"I didn't mean to step on your dress." Tears cover Luke's eyes.

Laura picks up a handful of the dress, rotates with measured movements, and kneels in front of Luke. "Of course, you didn't."

Luke cries. "I wanted a perfect day for you and pa."

"Today is perfect. I'm marrying the man I love and getting three children. Everything is fine."

"You sure?" Luke says.

Laura puts Luke's fear aside by handing him her bouquet. She pulls the ripped edge of the dress toward her and puts the fabric between her teeth. Laura tugs the destroyed lace from the dress.

"Here, Father." She hands a foot of shredded lace to him. "Please put this in your pocket." She places her hands on Luke's shoulders. "We both ripped the dress. I'll repair the hem later."

Luke straightens and wipes away tears. Laura gives him a quick hug.

Laura grasps her father's arm and pulls herself up. Luke hands her the flowers, and Laura faces the front. Luke picks up the train once more. The music resumes, and Laura places her hand in the crook of her father's arm.

Laura and her father stop in front of Pastor Johnston. After dropping the train, Luke sidesteps around the material and stands on the other side of Martha.

"Who gives this woman to be married?" Pastor Johnston looks at Mr. White.

"I do." Mr. White kisses Laura on the cheek. He sits with his wife on the pew across the aisle from Grandpa Joseph and Grandma Kay.

Pastor Johnston looks from the bride to the groom. "Love is patient, although with three children, patience will become a necessity in your home." He glances at the children standing by their father. "Laura has lived among us for the past nine years. She has lived with the Wards, taught school with Edward, and helped him with his children." The pastor grins. "A few of us prodded Edward to pursue Laura."

"I had planned on courting her." Edward winks at Laura.

"Their friendship blossomed into a deep love for each other. I am certain God has already blessed them, and I pray for continued blessings for them as a couple and a family." Pastor Johnston reads Scripture on marriage and remarks on the meaning of the verses. "Now, we will have a song by Edward's nieces."

Amos's daughters—Lizzie, Deborah, and Suzy, ranging in age from seventeen to twenty—rise, walk up the altar steps, and stand behind the pianist. After the introductory notes, Lizzie sings a verse from a love ballad. As the words flow along the calming breeze from the open windows, folks listen and watch the couple gazing into each other's eyes.

A gust of wind sweeps through the windows and ruffles several hats on ladies' heads. A buzzing noise disturbs the singing.

Laura glances down at her bouquet. A bee flies out. She tosses the flowers on the floor. Luke yells. Martha scurries next to her father. James leaps closer and examines the flowers.

Uh-oh. I hope no one gets stung.

Edward's eyes widen. "Boys, step back."

The girls stop singing when Edward darts around shooing the bee away. James and Luke flap their hands to assist him. The bee flies between Laura and the preacher.

Pastor Johnston whacks at the bee with his Bible. Laura twists and trips. The preacher drops the Bible. He catches Laura. Martha dashes to Grandma Kay's lap. Edward sprints to help Laura.

Undaunted, the bee zips toward the singers.

The pianist jumps up banging the notes of the piano and rushes down the three steps toward the pews for safety.

"Luke, leave the bee alone," Edward shouts. The boys stop chasing the flying insect and step back. The bee buzzes over the heads of the three singers who wave their hands and arms.

"Watch out," Lizzie yells and follows the pianist.

"Be still, Suzy," Deborah exclaims. "The bee's in your hair."

The oldest girl pulls at her hair while turning in circles. Concerned, Amos lurches from his seat to assist his daughter. Suzy's beau jerks up out of his seat to lend a hand. Deborah escapes from the chaos.

"Hold still," Amos says to Suzy.

"I can't." Suzy pulls at her hair.

Amos grabs Suzy's arm and pulls, but her hand is twisted in her hair along with the buzzing bee.

Suzy jumps in small circles. "Get the bee out of my hair!"

"I'm trying." Amos's hands are in her wild, tangled hair.

Shocked silence descends over the congregation. Laura and Edward stare at the men and Suzy. Pastor Johnston stands wide-eyed frozen in place.

"I can't get my hand on him," her beau says.

"Try harder." Suzy cries out.

Amos grabs her hair where the buzzing sounds and yanks.

"Ouch," Suzy yells.

"Owwww." Amos shakes his hand and drops a lock of hair. "The bee stung me."

"There, on the floor." The beau points downward, and Amos stomps the bee beneath his boot.

Amos, a disheveled Suzy, and her beau halt all movement. They stand facing the congregation. Reserved men and women attempt to stifle their chuckles. They fail. Sharp barks of laughter erupt. Young boys howl with amusement. Children giggle.

"I'm a mess." Suzy bursts into tears. Her curled brown hair is now a web of confusion.

Her beau sends her a shaky smile. "You're beautiful to me."

Suzy grabs her head where her father yanked her hair. Amos makes an attempt at consoling his daughter with an arm around her shoulders. Suzy will have none of her father's efforts. "Mother."

Thank goodness, her mother comes to the rescue.

"I know. Let's go get you cleaned up." Amos's wife escorts their daughter from the church with Amos right behind them.

"Sorry for the disruption," Amos says toward the bridal party.

Edward struggles at holding back chuckles. "It ... it's okay."

Laura stares after her soon-to-be niece and erupts into laughter with the preacher and Edward following her lead.

"A first for me." Preacher Johnston stoops and picks up the Bible.

"Does God want us to get married today?" Edward questions.

"I ... uh ... I hope so," Laura says.

James and Luke walk back and stand in their original places. Martha remains with her grandma.

The minister holds the closed Bible in one hand down by

his side. "I'm going to rush through this before anything else happens to stop this wedding. If anyone can show just cause why this man and woman should not be joined together, let him speak now or forever hold his peace."

Pastor Johnston scans the crowd. Folks in the audience glance around, waiting to see if there will be any more disruptions. The bride and groom sneak a glance at their audience, and when no one utters a word, they sigh. Relief washes over me too. I want the couple married once and for all.

The pastor resumes the ceremony.

Not two minutes later, James looks toward the aisle. "Paaaaa."

"Not now, son."

"Too late." James throws up his arms when his three-year-old cousin, Ezekiel, stands in the center of the aisle near the pew in front of me with chocolate frosting covering his mouth and hands. Ezekiel races down the aisle toward the front where the wedding party stands. Folks stare wide-eyed with mouths agape.

"This wedding cannot get any better." Mr. Obadiah Ward chuckles, and Sarah hushes him.

Laura's eyes widen. Edward's jaw drops. Pastor Johnston's eyes dart from the bride to the groom to Ezekiel. Two steps from the altar, Edward, James, and Luke jump to block Ezekiel from going any further. All three collide with each other and fall. When Ezekiel slips through an opening between Edward and James, he lunges for Laura. She attempts to step back but to no avail. Ezekiel grabs Laura around her legs in a messy hug.

Martha squeals. "Your dress."

All movement in the church stops. I fear Laura will burst into sobs when she surprises us all and burst into giggles. Laura grabs Ezekiel's chocolate-covered hand at the precise moment his out-of-breath mother halts midway down the aisle, her apron covered in chocolate.

Uh-oh, there goes the wedding cake.

Ezekiel's mother glares at her son. "You're in big trouble, young man."

"Hold on, everyone." Laura glances from Ezekiel's mother, over the congregation, and to Edward. "I want to get married." Edward nods and to the preacher, she says, "Today, if possible." She looks at Ezekiel. "You stand right here. Do not move." The boy obeys, and she releases Ezekiel's hand. His mother kneels in the aisle and waits.

Edward and his sons return to their previous positions, and Edward motions with a hand. "Pastor, get to the 'I dos', please."

The pastor continues, "The rings, please."

"Here." Edward reaches into his coat pocket, pulls out the wedding rings, and places them on top of the preacher's Bible. The pastor says a few words about wedding bands.

"Laura, do you take Edward to be your lawfully wedded husband?"

"I do." Laura licks chocolate from her fingers and holds out her hand. Edward picks up her band and slips the gold ring on her finger.

"Do you take Laura White to be your lawfully wedded wife?"

"I do." Edward grins, and the pastor hands a band to Laura who places the ring on Edward's finger.

"About time." Obadiah grins.

"By the power vested in me, I now pronounce you husband and wife. You may—"

Edward does not wait. He wraps his arms around Laura and kisses her. The crowd claps. Several of the men and boys whistle and hoot. Ezekiel's mother points at him indicating he needs to come to her right now. With a quivering lip, Ezekiel walks toward his mother.

Martha sticks her tongue out at Ezekiel when he walks past her. Ezekiel's mother grabs his hand, and they head toward the exit. Martha leaves her grandma, walks to Laura, and waits for her father to release Laura. "Can I call you Mama, now?"

Laura pauses, looks down at Martha, and tears fill her eyes. "This is the happiest day of my life."

Several women sniff and wipe their eyes with handkerchiefs.

"What about all the interruptions during our wedding?" Edward says.

"The bee was funny." Martha grins. "But I didn't want to get stung."

"I'm sure our marriage will have oodles of interruptions." Laura takes Martha's hand in hers. "And with these three children, there's never going to be a dull moment in our home."

"For certain." Edward's face beams with love for his new wife. "And ..." he looks at the three children and pulls Laura closer, "funny memories were made here today. A day we will remember forever."

"Amens" sound from a few people in the congregation.

Pastor Johnston places a hand on Edward's shoulder. "Other brides would have been in tears with chocolate handprints all over their wedding dress, and a ceremony interrupted by a bee. Remember this day, because life is short." The minister gazes at Edward's children and back to the couple. "Make memories. These children will be grown and married in a few years."

"I don't want to get married." Luke puffs out his chest. "Girls are silly. They don't like worms."

"Me either." Martha scrunches up her face.

Edward chuckles and looks at Luke. "You don't say. In about six years, I'll remind you of those words."

"Let's go eat." James aims for the front doors, and Luke races after his brother. With the teddy bear still in her arms, Martha wedges between Edward and her new mama.

Behind them the minister says, "Oh ...we forgot to light the unity candle."

"Too late." Edward calls over his shoulder. "The way this wedding has gone, I'm afraid we'd set the church on fire."

"Good point," the preacher acknowledges. "We attempt to make all the plans we want, but 'tis much funnier when God allows them to go awry."

"Now," Edward says, "let's get through the reception."

"Yes." Pastor Johnston nudges the couple, and they begin their descent down the aisle. He addresses the congregation. "Once the happy couple exits, you all follow us outside where refreshments await us under the pavilion."

When Laura steps near me, I hear her say to Edward, "Wonder what the cake looks like?"

Even though the marriage of Edward Thatcher and Laura White had been in the making before they were born, God allowed His plan to come to fruition as He saw fit—with a teddy bear, a bee, and a chocolate-covered little boy. One of the funniest and most interrupted weddings I have ever seen at Pumpkin Creek United Church.

7

1919: A VETERAN'S BURDEN

On a quiet Tuesday morning, the front door creaks open. The intruder shuts the door. A gentle click reverberates throughout the empty sanctuary. Lopsided footsteps wander down the church aisle, and wounded, World War I veteran, Larry Brown stops next to my eleventh pew position. He steps into my row, reaches for the pew in front of him, and takes a load off his body by sitting. With hands in lap, he stares forward.

"Why?" Weariness hangs in the air and around Larry's slumped shoulders.

I have found 'why' the most asked question among humans in despair.

"I should be thankful …"

Since returning from the war, today is the first time Larry has set foot in Pumpkin Creek United Church. Larry's older brother, Jacob Brown, requested prayer for Larry while he served our country. Jacob still requests prayer for his brother. According to Jacob, war affects more than the outer shell of a man leaving the mind full of turmoil. I hope Larry hands the burdens he carries over to God.

"I hate who I am. Look at me." Larry snaps the black eye patch covering his right eye. "You allowed this to happen. Sometimes I wished You had let me die." He leans forward with elbows on legs, tears falling on old work pants held up by a leather belt with extra holes poked into the strip taking up the slack.

After spending months at Walter Reed General Hospital, Jacob and wife, Maggie, drove up north and brought Larry back home. At the hospital, Jacob learned about the battle that injured Larry.

In June of 1918, the Battle of Belleau Wood occurred where American, French, and British forces fought against the Germans. Numerous comrades of Larry's were injured or killed by the enemy. Early one morning, machine guns fired, and trees exploded in the forest. Wood shards became shooting arrows through the forest, and Larry's body received the trauma. Larry woke in a US military base hospital where a fellow soldier had told the battle's story and how the forest looked as if shredded to pieces but was free of Germans.

Larry's homecoming was not what Jacob, Maggie, and their children, Eli and Becky, expected. Before the war, Larry and Eli were joined at the hip, now a huge gap separates the two.

"I killed men. I watched the life leave their bodies." Larry pauses, clenching his fist. "The screams of men in agony, I hear every night. The fear of death in their eyes, I still see in my nightmares. How do I go on?" Sobbing, Larry smacks the pew. If I were human, I would have recoiled.

Perhaps a good cry will do Larry good. Humans say crying cleanses the soul. However, from lessons and sermons I have heard innumerable times, God heals the heartbroken.

The front door opens and closes again. Odd, because Tuesdays are slow around here.

Joseph Thatcher walks into the sanctuary humming "Amazing Grace." With snow-white hair contrasting with a tan face from years of working outside at the sawmill, he wears a worn shirt and denim overalls. He stops up short when he sees Larry. Joseph clears his throat.

Larry jerks upright, pulls a handkerchief from a pocket, wipes his face, and sticks the cloth back in the pouch before he faces the individual.

Joseph greets Larry with a smile. "I see you found my favorite pew." He points at the seat next to Larry. "Mind if I join you?"

Not giving Larry time to respond, Joseph side-steps into my row, grasps the pew in front of me, and with slow movements, sits beside Larry, knee joints cracking like all those children who pop their knuckles during a church service. Larry slides over a good two feet.

"I'm not much company, Mr. Thatcher."

"I understand."

Larry frowns. "You do?"

Joseph crosses sturdy arms over the bib of the overalls. "I was a soldier in the Civil War."

"I didn't know that."

Larry had lived here a couple of years before he joined to fight in the war, thus he is not acquainted with all the Thatcher history as I am.

Larry looks him up and down. "You survived. I don't see any wounds." Joseph faces Larry and points at the cheek displaying a thin, red line under an unshaven face. "What happened?"

"A fight among us prisoners of war." Joseph grimaces. "One man loathed my witnessing and talking about Jesus all the time.

He had a piece of glass and used the shard against my face. I threw in a few good punches, though." He lifts his brows. "Not that fighting was the answer, but I had to defend myself."

"I don't know if I would have survived being a prisoner."

"I'd like to believe you would have." Joseph settles back against me. "God has been good to me. You see the one scar on the outside, doesn't mean I didn't suffer." He points at his head. "Up here." Then, points to his heart. "And in here."

Larry twists, places an elbow on the top of my pew back, and faces Joseph.

"My older brother, John Michael, and I were in prison together. Horrible. I wouldn't wish the place on my worst enemy. God watched over us." Joseph rubs the scar. "Like He watched over you."

"I suppose so."

"Sure, He did. You're home, surrounded by those who love you. I'm certain Jacob, Maggie, and the children prayed for you every day." Joseph points at his chest. "I did too."

"I know they love me. I love them." Larry adjusts the eye patch. "Look at me. I'm lost. I don't recognize who I am anymore."

"I didn't have the physical wounds you have, but I saw men with much worse. John Michael and I were glad to be alive and at home. Mother called us scrawny."

"Like me."

"Yep." Joseph chuckles. "The first week back home, Mother stayed in her kitchen cooking all day. Three hearty meals a day with all the cake and pie we could eat." He pats his stomach. "She said she was going to fatten us up. She did too."

"Maggie cooks all my favorites."

"One Sunday after the morning service, Eli told me how Maggie cooks your favorite dishes, and you don't eat much." Joseph eyes Larry. "Jacob said you stay shut up in your room."

Joseph rubs his left shoulder before stuffing a hand in the front pocket of the overalls. "Eli said you're not thankful for what his dad and mama do for you. I hope you realize, he misses fishing and joking around with you."

Larry frowns. "He said that?"

"Yep." The word pops from Joseph's mouth.

"I'm thankful." Larry fiddles with the eyepatch strap. "I ... getting back into a normal life is hard right now."

"Let Jacob and Maggie know. Eli misses your relationship with him. He used to follow you around like a puppy."

"He did." Larry sighs. "If he knew the things I did in the war. The men I harmed and killed."

"Larry, in war, a man fights. Kill or be killed." Joseph stretches out old legs. "You're a strong, young man. The human instinct is to survive. We're going to fight to the bitter end to save our life, the lives of our children, and in my case, my grandchildren."

"I would fight for Eli and Becky."

"Did you start the war?"

"No, sir."

"You're beating yourself up for something you didn't start. I didn't start the Civil War. Soldiers follow orders, do things they're not proud of or understand." Joseph exhales. "I did."

Larry mulls over Joseph's words. "How do I move on with my life?"

"Time. Prayer. I spent many hours with God down by the river. I fished and told Him everything. I couldn't keep the anger and resentment bottled up inside any longer. Things of that nature will drive a man crazy. I told God about all my evil thoughts. The hatred and bitterness I carried in my heart and mind. The things I did."

"That's how I feel. I'm going crazy."

"Tell Him." With a calloused index finger, Joseph points

heavenward. "Memories would hit me at the oddest times. Even with others around me, I'd be lost in my own horrible thoughts." He hesitates. "The nightmares were the worst."

"I have them too."

Joseph reaches for the pew in front of him shifting his body a tad. "Amos, my Father's best friend, took me on at the sawmill which was a gift from God. The exhaustive work helped me sleep better at night. But there were days when I questioned why God would allow war to happen." Joseph stretches out his left elbow.

"You okay, Mr. Thatcher?"

"Old age. I guess my arthritis is acting up."

On most days when Joseph visits, he sits with hands in his lap and eyes closed praying. Although Larry is here, Joseph appears restless. I hope all is well with him.

"I persevered," Joseph says. "You will too."

Today is the most I have ever heard Joseph speak about his time in the war and prison. I wished I could have helped him after he returned home.

Joseph asks, "Are you a believer in our Savior, Jesus Christ?"

"Yes, sir." Larry straightens. "I haven't been a good Christian though. Look at how I'm treating my family. I don't attend church services, pray, or read my Bible. I can't talk about the things I did and saw in the war."

"At first, I didn't share my war experiences with Father or my wife, Kay. Most were terrible recollections. Time is the cure." Joseph stretches his neck from side to side.

"You sure you're okay, Mr. Thatcher?"

"Nothing to worry about. A little winded and stiff this morning is all."

Arthritis. Winded. Stiff. This does not sound like the

Joseph I know and love. I hope he is not ill. Although, Joseph is getting up there in age.

Joseph continues, "As I talked with God and matured in my walk with Him, the brokenness in me healed. Memories do not pierce my mind as they did when I arrived home. In the end, I shared bits and pieces with others. I hope what I learned from my time in the war helps others." He smiles at Larry. "I cannot remember the last time I had a nightmare."

"Getting through my struggles will take time. I'm not a patient man." Larry rubs a scarred hand over his thigh. "I hope God forgives me."

"He will. You need to forgive yourself." After a few silent moments, Joseph asks, "Were Abraham, Moses, and King David believers?"

Larry nods.

"Look at what they did." Joseph forms a fist and sticks out the index finger. "One, Abraham had a child by another woman after God told him Sarah would have a child." He straightens the middle finger. "Two, Moses killed a man." Joseph adds the third finger. "Three, David plotted and had Uriah killed." He sticks his hand back in the overalls pocket. "Did God forgive them?"

Larry nods again.

"God forgave me for all the wrong I did in the war, my evil thoughts and my actions. He forgave Abraham, Moses, and David. Do you think your sins and problems are too big for our Almighty God to handle?"

"No, sir." Larry glances downward and back at Joseph. "I guess I didn't consider those men, their sins, and the way God used them."

"Remember." Joseph turns in the seat toward Larry. "Being a Christian doesn't mean you're not going to sin. You'll sin until the day you die." He smiles. "The more I've grown in my walk with God, the more I'm aware of my obedience or disobedience to Him. You only find the answers in the Word. That's why I read the Scriptures every day and pray."

Why do humans always try to solve everything first on their own before going to God? Will they ever learn?

"I don't understand war, Mr. Thatcher, or why God let me live."

Joseph exhales a slow breath. "Have you read the Bible?"

"Not the entire Book."

"There has been war since the beginning of time. Look at everything the Israelites went through in the Old Testament. Yet God kept them alive because His Son would be a descendent all the way down through King David. Remember, David went through loads of trials and tribulations." Joseph glances at the cross on the wall and back toward Larry. "Because humans have volition, we don't always do what's right in God's sight. There will be wars and rumors of wars until Jesus comes back. Your war was not the last one. There will be wars after you and I are gone."

"I don't wish war on anyone."

"None of us would. His ways and His plans are not always our ways." Again, Joseph points heavenward.

"I guess so."

"Don't be a doubting Thomas."

Larry chuckles. What a nice sound to hear from him.

"God has worked a multitude of miracles in my life. I'm here today because of Him. I've been blessed with seventy-seven years on this earth. Did you know I had a close call with death when I was twelve?"

"No, sir."

Joseph recounts the story of when he had yellow fever.

"You were healed?" Larry's left eye widens.

"Yes. God had a purpose for me. I hope I have fulfilled

what He wanted me to do." Joseph taps the aisle side of my armrest. "Look here." Both men stand, move into the aisle, and face the plaque attached to my armrest. They pause a few seconds and return to their seats. "The plate commemorates what God did for me. Lightning struck the oak tree in our front yard. Now, we're sitting on the pew made from the tree."

To this day, I am not fond of storms. At least, I do not get drenched in the rain anymore.

Larry's mouth twitches upward into a slight smile. "You don't look as if you were ever sickly, Mr. Thatcher."

Joseph grins. "I have been blessed beyond my wildest dreams. I survived the war, had godly parents, a good wife, children, beautiful grandchildren, health, a home, job, and plenty to eat."

"Before I went to war, Eli and I pulled tons of pranks on Maggie and Becky. Seems we were always in trouble with them."

"He misses you." Joseph adjusts the overalls' left strap. "I bet they all do."

Joseph touches his left shoulder again. I have the strangest feeling all is not well with him.

Pangs of guilt wash over Larry's face. "How did the war change you?"

"After we returned, my brother became a preacher, I worked at the sawmill with Amos, who became my father-in-law. Amos said the boards I worked with received the brunt of my anger and frustration. The work was God's way of allowing me to let go of my demons."

"What do you mean?"

"Better to take out my frustration and bitterness on a piece of wood than my family and friends. The physical labor left me exhausted, I dropped into bed every night. Over time, my nightmares faded." Joseph chokes up. "If hell is like the prison ..."

Larry rakes a hand through unkempt hair. "I'm a prisoner in my own mind."

"In our prison," Joseph rubs the scruff on his chin, "death was everywhere. The sounds of grown men crying and screaming while death overtook them. Sometimes, I wanted to die."

"I ..." Unshed tears form in Larry's left eye. "I hear their screams every night when I close my eyes."

Joseph hesitates before he recounts his time in prison. "Filth was all around us. Rats and insects crawled around eating human flesh." Joseph shudders. "God showed favor on us like He did Daniel. I knew I needed to serve God wherever I was. He never promised me an easy path, but the guards allowed John Michael to preach and me to sing." A faraway look shines in Joseph's eyes. "Sometimes I'd watch the guards. They listened to John Michael. You never know the seed God will allow you to plant."

"I doubt I planted any seeds."

Joseph arches an eyebrow. "Not too late. God allowed you to come home. Plant seeds in your nephew."

Larry shrugs. "I guess I should try."

"I will never forget a man named Warren." Joseph glances over at Larry, his expression solemn. "The prisoners and guards watched Warren jerk and scream through his torment. He laid on a mat on the floor. Warren's wound was infected, and the smell reeked. John Michael and I prayed and witnessed to him. He was angry with God." Joseph swipes at an eye. "Darkness surrounded Warren."

Joseph pauses, and Larry remains silent waiting for him to finish the story. I ache for the pain Joseph suffered in the prison.

"Sometimes, the other prisoners suggested Warren yelled at Satan himself." Sadness overtakes Joseph's face. "I don't know who he saw or yelled at, but the experience was frightening. Before dusk, the dank barrack went pitch black, and a piercing shriek sounded around us. A guard lit a lantern and slid the light between the barred doors for us. Horror filled Warren's eyes."

Larry leans inward toward Joseph. I long to hear what Joseph will say next knowing his words cannot be good.

"John Michael shouted at Warren. I shook him hard trying to get his attention. The man was hysterical." Joseph swallows. "Warren's nails gripped into my arms. He yelled at us to make his anguish stop. We couldn't. We didn't see anything. A cold gust swept over and around us. John Michael and I felt the coolness hover over Warren. A deafening shrill escaped from Warren right before he gasped his last breath." Joseph shivers. "He left for a world of torture and total separation from God. I believe Warren saw what was in store for him." Joseph looks away lost in the memory. "Out of everything I saw in the war, his death was the most terrifying."

"He died," Larry pauses, "and went to hell?"

Joseph nods, swiping at his watery eyes. "Warren told us he would never believe in a God who allowed this war and devastation to happen. Thinking about the nightmare now gives me goosebumps." He holds an arm out showing Larry. "John Michael shared the gospel with the prisoners and guards again. Seven men, including the guards, put their trust in Christ. God put us in the prison for His purpose."

"Whew." Larry shivers. "The story gives me goosebumps too."

"In spite of everything we went through in our wars, nothing will be as horrifying as being sent to hell." Joseph hesitates. "The prison and Warren—a time I'll never forget."

"Thanks for sharing your time in prison with me."

"You experienced things in the war you'll never share with another living soul. Give God your suffering and pain. Take one day at a time. Make sure you use your time on earth to glorify Him. God brought you back home for a reason. Be the godly uncle Eli and Becky deserve. Work your farm serving God, not man." Joseph puts a hand on Larry's shoulder. "He will lead you where He wants you. Pray without ceasing and search the Scriptures for answers. God's Word will give you a peace which surpasses all understanding."

"You believe God put you in the prison for His purpose?"

"Without a doubt. I want my last breath and actions on earth to be serving Him when He calls me home."

The church door clangs open. "Uncle Larry." Eli bursts into the church and down the aisle.

Larry jerks up, pivots, and beams at the boy.

"Hi, Eli." Larry glances down at Joseph. "I need to talk to him, Mr. Thatcher. Eli and I had words before I came here." Joseph shifts, and Larry passes by him into the aisle. He ambles a step toward Eli, and they meet one pew behind me. Joseph slides down my seat away from the pair and gives them privacy.

"Uncle Larry, I'm sorry." The words rush from Eli's mouth.

"No, no. Everything's my fault. I am going through pain and sorrow. I shouldn't be taking my problems out on you or our family."

Eli's eyes go wide. "So, we'll hang around with each other? Go fishing?"

"Yep." Larry hugs his nephew. "Let's say good-bye to Mr. Thatcher and head back home."

Larry and Eli turn around in time to see Joseph stand and grip a hand over his heart. With his face creased in pain, Joseph slumps down on me.

Larry and Eli hurry over beside Joseph, but I see there is no use. Joseph's time has passed. He performed his last act of service to the Lord by sharing how God helped him through his war experience with a veteran in need. I am honored to have been a witness to Joseph and Larry's conversation.

From the deepest depths of my being, I am grieved for I will never see or hear Joseph Everett Thatcher again. As always, only God knows the amount of time He gives each human. I hope, each human is ready when He calls.

8

1927: FLOYD "FAST-HAND" OWENS

"*D*runkenness is of the devil. Stay away from the filth." Our new preacher, Phil Rowe, spoke the words, not twenty minutes ago, during the sermon. He said inebriation was another way Satan pierced his hooks into mankind.

The word is, law enforcement officials have blockades set up all over the county as they chase one Floyd "Fast-Hand" Owens, a bootlegger on the run. The gossipmongers say he carries a gun and, from the reports of apprehended criminal associates, is fast to pull the weapon for no apparent reason. At the conclusion of this morning's service, Preacher Rowe prayed the congregation would avoid the snares of alcohol and Floyd would be captured with no one hurt.

After most of the congregation headed outside, a small group lingers inside the church. A crisp, autumn breeze blows through the open windows and front door. Hearty male laughter mixes with the ladies' soft voices and the children's high-pitched giggles.

"Are you all right, Mama?" Five-year-old Katie holds her baby doll by the arm where the toy dangles by her side.

Pregnant with her second child, Ethel Thatcher rubs her belly. "I'll be fine."

"Are you sure, honey?" Suzanne Ward stares at Ethel's waistline. "I do believe the baby's ready to come."

At thirty-nine-years-old, Suzanne became pregnant, and God blessed her and Benjamin with a son, Jackson.

"According to Dr. Perkins," says James, Ethel's husband, "she has a couple more weeks."

I cannot believe James is grown, married, and has a second child on the way. As clear as yesterday, I recall the wedding of James's father and Laura. Both stood at the front of the church while the groom swatted a bee.

"I hope he's right." Suzanne lifts an eyebrow. "You remember, Jackson was early. The delivery wasn't easy."

"We remember, Suzanne." Seventy-eight-year-old Grandmother Kay's blue eyes shine behind bifocals. "From the way Ethel looks, I say she's ready to have the baby."

"I hope so. He's a kicker." Ethel frowns inhaling a deep breath.

Fourteen-year-old Jackson Ward runs into the sanctuary and stops beside his mother. "Father asked that you come on. He's hungry. Ready for lunch."

Suzanne smiles at her son. "I'm on my way." She looks at Ethel. "You need to relax."

Grandmother Kay pats Ethel's shoulder. "I'll stay with you this afternoon and watch Katie, so you can rest."

"How is everyone today?" Preacher Rowe, medium build and clean cut, joins the small group lingering after the service.

The preacher joined the church earlier in the year. As far as I see, he is a man who preaches the Word. During the winter of 1918, pneumonia seized Pastor Jeremiah Johnston, and the Lord took him home. The next pastor, Reverend Doyle, lasted seven years until his wife's death. I predict Preacher Rowe will last years at Pumpkin Creek United Church.

James places a hand under his wife's elbow. "Ethel's been more tired the last two days."

The preacher shakes Grandmother Kay's hand and looks at Ethel and James, "I'm excited we'll have another child in our congregation soon. I love seeing our church families grow."

Beyond the open front door, sirens wail. Automobile engines clunk and thump across the churchyard. Fathers and mothers roar at their children to get out of the way. Women and children yell and scream. In the distance, a gun blasts.

Suzanne shrieks. Grandmother Kay slaps a hand over her chest. Ethel and James whip their heads toward the front door. James scoops Katie into his arms.

Tires screech to a halt in the churchyard.

Outside, a boy yells. "They shot the tire out. Run. He's getting out of the truck."

Automobile doors clang open. Authoritative male voices boom.

"The man has a gun." A man's voice rises.

Feet pound the church grounds.

"Get outta my way." A man with loud footsteps bounds up the church steps.

"What's going on?" Preacher Rowe runs toward the vestibule and halts when the man enters the church with a gun pointed at the preacher's chest. Preacher Rowe sticks both hands up. "Whoa, there."

The man demands, "Back up, away from the door." The preacher steps forward. The man pushes the pastor. "Now."

Oh no. Not good.

James pulls Ethel closer. Katie wraps her arms around her

father's neck. Suzanne, Jackson, and Grandmother Kay stare wide-eyed at the intruder.

"You heard me." The man points the gun toward the sanctuary, slams, and bolts the front door.

"Everyone away from the church. Now." An officer's voice bellows on the other side of the barred door. "Men, surround the building."

Benjamin Ward shouts, "My wife and son are inside."

"Grandmother Kay, Ethel, and Katie are too," a teenager yells.

"Everyone back away from the door and windows." The officer's voice is loud and demanding. "Floyd Owens is armed and dangerous."

The voices from outside fade. Floyd runs near the edge of a window and glances out. He jerks back.

A big man with broad shoulders under a worn, brown jacket, Floyd is tall—over six feet. He wears a dark hat and from what is visible, has brown, cropped hair. Floyd's dusty, brown shoes have seen better days.

Katie whimpers. Grandmother Kay grips my seat back. Pastor Rowe steps between her and Floyd.

An officer calls out, "You're surrounded."

Jackson's eyes widen. "Are you—"

With a pale face, Suzanne grasps Jackson's arm. "Be quiet. Do as he says."

Floyd bellows, "Everyone, sit down."

James, Ethel, and Katie plop down on me with Katie squeezed between her parents. I remain on the left side, eleventh pew. Grandmother Kay edges onto the pew behind me, and the preacher sits next to her. Suzanne and Jackson drop down on the pew in front of me.

There goes my quiet Sunday afternoon.

"Oh, my back." Ethel grimaces.

"Is she having a baby?" Floyd's eyes widen.

"Soon." James rubs Ethel's shoulder.

Jackson twists around in the seat. "The notorious Floyd 'Fast-Hand' Owens is in our church."

"Jackson." Suzanne glares hard at her son.

"All of you hush up." Floyd paces around darting worried eyes toward the windows.

The law enforcement officer uses a bullhorn. "Floyd, come out with your hands up."

"I can't believe you're here, Fast-Hand." Jackson bounces on the seat.

Floyd keeps an eye on everyone. He crosses the aisle opposite the others and plops down onto a pew still facing the hostages. The gun remains in his right hand. He does not resemble a hardened criminal although looks are deceiving.

With innocence in her eyes, Katie tilts her head. "Why're you fast hand?"

"He carries a gun," Jackson says. "I bet you pull the weapon on all those men you do business with. Can you outdraw them, Fast-Hand?"

"Hush your mouth," Suzanne snaps.

"Are you going to shoot every one of us?" Preacher Rowe says.

"Hush up, preacher man." Floyd scowls at the preacher and waves the gun. "I ain't killed nobody. The gun's for protection."

"Have you ever been shot?" Jackson asks. Suzanne yanks him back.

"You do work among criminals, Mr. Owens." Grandmother Kay pulls her shawl tighter around her shoulders. "I suspect you do need protection. However, we aren't going to harm you."

"I understand that, ma'am, but I need to protect myself, my interests. I pull my gun if the situation gets dicey. A few criminals have tried to short-change me. I ain't having none of that. The men I work for would shoot me if I didn't bring back their money from the deliveries."

"Are you what they call a runner, Mr. Floyd?" Jackson's eyes widen.

"Yep." Floyd glances at the boy. "Drivin' comes natural to me." He glances around the sanctuary. "I'm no good at farmin' or books."

"I wouldn't try to steal from you." Jackson shakes his head.

"Ow." Ethel reaches for the small of her back.

"Hold up on the baby, ma'am. That's the last thing I need right now."

"I don't have any say in the matter." Ethel blows out a hard breath.

"Floyd, I know you hear me." The officer bellows. "Are you coming out or do we bust down the door?"

James stretches upward and peers out the window nearest him. "They mean business."

Preacher Rowe smacks the pew. "Let the women and children go."

"Hold on." Floyd rubs the scruff on his jaw. "I need to get my thoughts together."

"Will he hurt us, Papa?" Katie snivels.

James pulls Katie onto his lap. "Sweetie, we'll be fine."

"I knew I shouldn't have done this last job. My wife begged me to stay home." Floyd whips off his hat and throws the cap on the pew beside him. "If he hadn't shot my tire out, I could've outrun him."

"You're married?" Suzanne glares at Floyd. "What sort of husband are you?"

"Tryin' to make a living." He points the gun between the preacher and James. "Like them. I got four younguns, and the money comes in handy."

Suzanne points at Floyd. "What you do is against the law."

"Mother, you and Father enjoy wine with dinner. Isn't wine alcohol?" Jackson frowns. Grandmother Kay chuckles.

"Hush." Suzanne blushes.

"He's got a point, ma'am." Floyd nods. "Men can make their own choice about drinking."

"From what I've witnessed, best not to indulge," Preacher Rowe says.

Floyd does not act the harden criminal I heard folks talk about, and his gaze softens when he looks at Katie and Ethel. Maybe he understands the unwise career choice he has made.

"James," Ethel grips her stomach and leans over. "The baby's coming sooner rather than later."

Jackson fidgets and glances around. "Miss Ethel's gonna have her baby at gunpoint."

"Jackson Ward, keep quiet," Suzanne demands before twisting around and facing Ethel. "Try lying down on the pew. Maybe the pain will ease off." Ethel leans against James, sighs, and lifts her legs onto my seat.

Grandmother Kay removes the shawl from around her shoulders, rises, and places a makeshift pillow behind Ethel's head. Grandmother Kay hovers, worry etched on her wrinkled face.

"Do you hear me, Floyd?" The officer demands.

"Preacher, go over to the window." Floyd points with the gun. "Tell him everything's under control then come right back and sit down."

Preacher Rowe obeys. "Everything is under control."

"Is anyone hurt?"

"No."

"Get back over here," Floyd demands, beckoning again with the gun.

"She needs the doctor," Suzanne says.

With a furrowed brow, Floyd rises and paces in the center aisle, still away from the windows. At least the gun is not pointed at anyone.

"Suzanne. Jackson. Are you okay?" Benjamin's voice hurries through a window. Jackson rushes over and waves at his father. The boy sees the situation as an adventure. I am sure, the adults disagree.

"Get back, sir," an authoritative voice orders Benjamin.

"Sit down now," Floyd commands. Jackson rushes to a seat.

Ethel pants and labors in pain. She rotates onto her side, but my wooden seat cannot be too comfortable for a pregnant woman.

"Grandmother Kay." James blinks in rapid succession. "Is the baby going to come now?"

Grandmother Kay places a hand on Ethel's stomach. Ethel's brow breaks out in beads of sweat.

"Hmmm." Grandmother Kay twitches her lips.

"Dear God, the pain." Ethel shrieks and clutches her abdomen.

Suzanne jerks up. "She needs a doctor."

"Floyd, if anything happens to her and the baby," Preacher Rowe says, "you will be held accountable."

"I'm going to the window and ask they fetch the doctor." Suzanne heads toward the window the pastor spoke from moments ago.

"No." Floyd gestures again with the gun. "You two ladies help her. Son, you go ask for the doctor and come right back."

Jackson dashes to a window. "We need Dr. Perkins. Mrs. Ethel's having her baby. Hurry."

"Today's turning out to be a disaster. My wife's gonna kill me." Floyd paces and swipes a sleeve over his brow.

"The police will get you first." Preacher Rowe yanks and loosens his tie.

"I never hurt anyone. This is gettin' out of hand. All I do is drive a truck and deliver whiskey." Floyd shakes his head and mumbles, "What am I gonna do?"

"I suggest you let us go," the pastor says.

"You said you never hurt anyone with the gun." Jackson looks hopeful.

"No, not yet. In my line of work, you meet thieves. I've heard the stories told about me. They've been exaggerated. I have the gun in case I need protection."

Jackson leans against a pew. "You're not a bad man, are you?"

Floyd stops pacing and considers the boy. "I don't think so, others might. You know what's funny? I don't drink the stuff."

"He breaks the law." Suzanne flashes hard eyes at Floyd before turning back to Ethel, opening her purse, and removing a monogrammed handkerchief which she hands to James. "Wipe her brow."

"That's true. I break the law." Floyd cuts eyes toward Preacher Rowe. "And I go to church."

Everyone stares at Floyd. I too am astonished at the admission.

"I'm glad to hear that," Preacher Rowe says.

"Why're you a runner?" Jackson asks.

"I can't farm worth two cents. I've tried. The bank foreclosed on our home and land." Floyd shrugs. "Besides, I stopped school at fifth grade."

The pastor says, "There has to be some other work you're capable of doing for a living."

"I do odd jobs when needed."

"Can we have your coat, Pastor?" Grandmother Kays says. "She needs her head lifted more."

The preacher removes his coat and hands the jacket over.

"Here." Floyd removes one arm from his jacket, transfers the gun to the other hand, and removes the coat.

"Thank you, Mr. Floyd." Katie's voice is soft. "My mama doesn't feel good."

"I know." He smiles at the little girl. "You're welcome."

James and Grandmother Kay fold the coats into makeshift pillows and position them behind Ethel's shoulders.

"Ouch." Ethel grabs her stomach and tears escape from her eyes. "The pain's sharp. Something's not right."

"Time her pains, James." Grandmother Kay feels Ethel's stomach again.

"What's wrong?" James' brow furrows.

"The baby's turned."

"What?" Ethel demands, trying hard to sit upright. "Is the baby all right?"

"Breech?" Floyd grimaces.

"Maybe." Grandmother Kay presses Ethel's stomach.

Suzanne stands. "How can I help?"

"Mama, Mama." Katie cries and drops her doll onto the floor.

James looks at Jackson. "Take Katie over to another pew please."

James hugs Katie and picks up her doll, handing the figurine to her before Jackson takes her hand. With tears rolling down Katie's cheeks, Jackson leads her across the aisle and near the front away from all the activity.

"Floyd, what're you going to do?" Preacher Rowe gestures toward Ethel. "Wait until something happens to her and the baby? You need to do what's right."

Floyd runs a hand over his hair. "I know, preacher. I don't want to lose my family either. If I go out there, I could get shot."

"You should've thought of that before you became a

runner." The pastor's face reddens. "You'll go to jail—if they don't shoot you."

"I see I done wrong."

"Owww," Ethel yells struggling to find comfort. "Help me."

"Lord, forgive me." Floyd hurries to where Ethel lies. "Preacher, find out why the doctor isn't here."

The pastor says, "Dr. Perkins attends the Presbyterian church, across the river."

"Shucks." Floyd exhales. "Ma'am, I could help you."

"You are joking." Suzanne puts her hands on her hips.

Grandmother Kay stares at Floyd. "How?"

Floyd places the gun beside him on the pew and rolls up his shirt sleeves. "I told y'all I wasn't much of a farmer. To make ends meet, sometimes I assisted the animal doc with the birth of farm animals, you know, cows and horses."

"Wait." Ethel's eyes widen. "I'm not an animal."

James rubs her shoulder. "He's here and able to help now, Ethel. Please give him a chance."

"Let Floyd feel your stomach." Grandmother Kay directs Ethel. "I'm old. The birth will take at least the two of us."

Ethel nods. Floyd places both hands on her upper belly and presses. His hands move over her lower belly.

"Breech." Floyd frowns. "I've done this before." Relief washes over Ethel's face before Floyd glances at her. "With a calf."

Grandmother Kay gasps. Suzanne places her hand over her heart. James rakes a hand through his hair and Ethel, poor Ethel, giggles, more tears rolling down her cheeks.

"He's all we have at the moment." Grandmother Kay pats Ethel's hand.

Floyd reaches into a pocket and pulls out a pocketknife. "Preacher, we're gonna need something to sterilize this and our hands." He hands the small knife to the pastor.

"Wait a minute." James squeezes Ethel's shoulders. "A knife."

"It'll be fine, James. He needs to cut the baby's cord," Grandmother Kay says.

"Oh, yeah." James relaxes.

Jackson reminds Floyd. "You have a truck load of whiskey. From my science studies, that'll sterilize anything."

"Good point." Preacher Rowe rushes to the window. "Get me whiskey from Floyd's truck and bring the bottles to the door." The preacher waves a hand. "Hurry, Ethel's having her baby."

Murmurs flow in through the windows from the police force and the members standing around the churchyard waiting to see what happens.

"You two." Floyd gestures at James and Suzanne. "Find whatever cloth you can." Floyd pauses for a moment. "You men, your shirts will work. Is there an outdoor pump?"

"Yes." Jackson stands and steps closer, leaving Katie sitting on the pew.

"Go get water and don't let anyone else come inside."

Jackson rips off a tweed Sunday coat and dress shirt leaving on a white T-shirt. He hands the clothing to Suzanne. The preacher and James do the same although James's T-shirt displays huge sweat stains at his armpits and around the neckline.

Floyd looks at Grandmother Kay. "Tear the shirts and wring them in the water he brings back. Keep Miss Ethel cool." With a hand, Floyd motions to the preacher. "Sir, keep those children over there." He glances at James. "She's gonna need you. Stay behind her head and shoulders. Keep her upper body up against yours. She'll need to push against you."

At the pounding on the front door, the preacher rushes and answers the door. Jackson steps inside and half-walks, half-runs down the center aisle sloshing water on the floor. Preacher Rowe grabs two whiskey bottles from the officer on the front steps, slams the door, and turns the deadbolt. The pastor rushes around pews, sets his sights on a window, and sticks agitated hands out over the windowsill. He uncaps the whiskey bottle, tilts the glass, and liquid splashes over both hands and the knife.

Grandmother Kay pours whiskey on a cloth and hands the rag to Floyd. He wipes both hands.

Floyd watches Ethel. "I'm gonna press and see if the baby moves. We don't want his feet coming out first."

Ethel pants through a contraction before the preacher hands the knife to Floyd.

James's face distorts in worry. "Will you need the knife?"

"If the baby's breech, there's the possibility I'll need to cut the baby out."

"No." Ethel cries.

"Maybe the doctor will get here soon." Floyd's words do not comfort Ethel, her face red and etched in pain.

"Ethel, let me and Suzanne help you get prepared." Grandmother Kay looks at Floyd who steps away. The ladies use grandma's shawl as a barrier from the others and prepare her for the birth. James consoles Ethel while the preacher and Floyd speak in hushed tones.

"Mama, Mama." Katie runs toward her mother. The preacher reaches for the little girl and pulls her into his arms.

"We're going to pray for your mama and the baby. Afterwards, we'll find you a pencil and paper. How about drawing a picture for your new brother or sister?"

"Okay," Katie utters through a hiccup. Jackson, the pastor, and Katie huddle together on the front pew away from the mother-to-be.

Ethel screams. "He has to come out."

"The contractions are less than sixty seconds apart." James darts his eyes around the sanctuary. "Where is Dr. Perkins?"

Grandmother Kay grips my pew back.

"Let me see." Floyd settles himself near Ethel's feet and places hands on her stomach. "Nothing."

"I have to push." Ethel leans up, her face scrunched and reddening.

"No. Breathe. The baby's not ready yet. Breathe."

Ethel inhales a sharp breath, leans back into James, and exhales.

"Ethel, I need to shift the baby, or we're gonna have to open you up. Do you understand?"

James rubs his wife's shoulder. "We understand."

"Miss Kay, Suzanne, I need you both pressing on her stomach."

Suzanne walks around, slides into my row, and kneels on the floor beside Ethel. Grandmother Kay leans further over my pew back ready to assist.

Floyd presses down hard. "Miss Kay, press inward on your side." When she does, Floyd presses and turns. "Suzanne, press near my pinkie finger and push upward."

"He moved." Suzanne smiles.

"Another ... contraction." Ethel wails.

"Quickly Miss Kay, push downward like you're rubbing her belly. Add pressure." Floyd presses upward from the bottom toward Ethel's left side.

Ethel pants in short breaths.

"I'm right here, honey." James holds Ethel up from behind her shoulders.

When the contraction subsides, Floyd presses a hand on Ethel's belly. "Whew, the baby turned. He's the right way."

"Praise the Lord." Suzanne exhales.

"Let me check the baby," Floyd says.

"Do what you need to do." Ethel slumps into her husband. "I can't take much more."

"You'll feel pressure from me." Floyd reaches into the birth canal. Ethel winces. "Miss Kay, I need cloth." He reaches for the rags.

Another contraction hits Ethel. She screams. Katie cries, and the preacher soothes her with soft whispers.

"Get ready, Ethel. When the contraction comes, push."

The contraction encompasses Ethel. She pushes with all her might.

"Breathe. You can't pass out on us. Breathe. I see the head," Floyd says. "Hold her firm, James. Push. Almost there." Floyd glances around.

"What's wrong?" Suzanne asks.

"I need something to wrap the baby in."

Within the tight space of my pew row, Suzanne stands and whips off her jacket. At the ready, Grandmother Kay holds a wet cloth to clean her great-grandchild.

Every feature on Ethel's face constricts.

"Push," Floyd commands, "push hard."

James holds his wife's upper body steady. Ethel wails.

Suzanne cheers. "Push, Ethel."

"You're doing great," Grandmother Kay smiles.

"One more push, Ethel." Floyd grabs Suzanne's jacket with one hand and places the decorative fabric under the newborn's body. "You have a boy."

Grandmother Kay hands Floyd the cloth. He wipes the baby's nose, mouth, and eyes. Once cleared, the baby wails to life, and Ethel collapses against James.

"Thank you, Lord." Grandmother Kay wipes tears from her eyes.

"Thank you," James says.

A proud great-grandmother, Kay, holds her arms out and

accepts the newborn from Floyd. He cuts the cord. After Ethel delivers the placenta, Floyd wipes his hands with the torn shirts and walks over where the pastor and the children sit. Grandmother Kay hands the baby to James. Then, the ladies assist Ethel.

An officer's voice rings through an open window. "Dr. Perkins is here."

"Too late." James grins and holds the baby near the window for all to see. The folks outside clap and cheer.

"Mama, Mama, I wanna see?" Katie runs to her parents.

"Meet your new little brother." James hands Ethel the baby. Katie lifts a finger and touches her brother's delicate features. Grandmother Kay remains near Ethel. Jackson stands at the window explaining what has transpired.

Floyd stands in the row behind me watching the family. Preacher Rowe comes up beside him and grasps a shoulder. "Good job."

"Thank you." The smile drops from Floyd's face. He looks down on me where he last placed the gun. Lifting his gaze, Floyd sees the gun in Suzanne's hand.

Pointing the gun at Floyd, Suzanne directs Jackson. "Go unlock the door and let the police inside."

Worry crosses Jackson's face. "Mother, please be careful."

I too worry her frazzled fingers will pull the trigger.

"I'll take that," Preacher Rowe says, and Suzanne lowers the gun.

When the preacher reaches for the gun, Floyd grabs and misses. The pastor grasps the handle. He pushes Floyd out of the way. Suzanne releases her grip. The pastor's finger catches the trigger.

Bang.

Floyd jumps back. The gun falls on the floor. The pastor snatches the gun up and scans the area.

"Anyone hurt?" The preacher darts quick glances at the others.

With eyes wide, James, Ethel, and Grandmother Kay shake their heads. Katie's hands cover her ears.

"Thank God." Suzanne sighs.

Floyd watches the pastor. Jackson rushes down the aisle with two officers running behind him.

"There he is." Jackson points, and Floyd raises both arms. A young officer rushes to secure Floyd's wrists in handcuffs.

"Who did he shoot? We heard gunfire." The taller officer looks around at everyone. "Y'all okay?"

The small group of hostages nod. The preacher says, "We're fine."

Katie walks down my row closer to the aisle, stops, and points. "The pew's been shot."

My goodness, I *have* been shot.

Suzanne clasps a hand over her mouth. Grandmother Kay lifts a wrinkled hand heavenward and says, "Praise God no one was killed."

The tall officer asks, "What happened?"

After explaining the incident with the gun, the pastor realizes the weapon is still in his hand. The preacher holds the gun out in the direction of the officer who grasps the weapon.

"Are the handcuffs necessary?" Preacher Rowe says.

"He's a fugitive." The taller man grimaces.

"Has he killed anyone?" the preacher lifts a brow.

"No, but he's a runner."

"He helped my mama." Katie bounces over, wraps her arms around Floyd's leg, and gives him a quick hug.

"Sure did. He delivered my son." James faces Floyd. "We cannot thank you enough."

"Floyd, you were a blessing today." Grandmother Kay clasps her hands together at her chest.

A well-dressed man carrying a black case walks into the church. "Someone sent for me."

"Dr. Perkins, over here." Suzanne points to the newborn. The doctor walks between a row of pews and comes around near the family. Ethel hands him her baby, and the doctor inspects the newborn.

"You need to look over here." Jackson points.

"Why?" The doctor lifts a brow.

Jackson snickers. "Preacher Rowe shot the pew." The doctor looks at me and chuckles.

"The gun slipped from our hands." Suzanne rushes an explanation.

"Take care of the baby and mother," the preacher says. "Everything's fine." Preacher Rowe looks at the policemen. "What will happen to Floyd?"

"Jail," the young officer answers in no uncertain terms.

"How long?" Jackson says.

"That's up to the judge."

"Where will you take him?" Pastor Rowe asks.

"Raleigh," the taller officer glances at the preacher, "where he'll await trial."

"Floyd, what you've been doing is wrong, but," Preacher Rowe shakes his head a time or two, "if the judge allows, I'll testify on your behalf and share what you did today."

Floyd nods, and the preacher grabs Floyd's hat and coat.

The younger officer nudges Floyd forward.

"Wait a minute," Ethel speaks up. "Thank you for all you did for me and our baby. God brought you here today because He knew I needed you." She glances at her husband. "I ... want to name him." James nods, and Ethel faces the men again. "Floyd Owen Thatcher."

Floyd glances down and up. "I'd be honored, ma'am."

Jackson blurts out, "Are you going to call him Fast-Hand?"

"Jackson." Suzanne raises her hands in an *I-give-up* gesture.

"Never," Grandmother Kay answers. "The pew built in honor of my dear, departed husband has been shot. We've had enough with the guns."

"Amen," Preacher Rowe says. The pastor pats Floyd on the shoulder. "We'll make sure your wife and kids are settled and have what they need."

"Y'all sure are nice to a man who held you at gunpoint."

Jackson stops beside Floyd. "You weren't going to hurt us, were you?"

"Never." Floyd smiles.

"We all make mistakes," the preacher says. "I hope you've learned your lesson."

"Yes, sir. Stay away from churches with pregnant ladies." Floyd grins. "Joking with you, Mrs. Ethel. If the judge doesn't kill me, my wife will."

The officers tip their hats to the ladies. The taller one prods Floyd. "Let's go." The fugitive leads the way with the officers and Preacher Rowe close behind.

"What a day." Jackson beams and notices his father striding into the sanctuary. Jackson glances at Suzanne. "I bet Father's starving."

"Me too," James says. "Can we go home, Doc?"

"Yes, I'll follow you all to your house and check on Ethel and the baby more thoroughly."

The small group gathers their belongings and head outside where the congregation awaits. I hear cheers, laughter, and ladies gushing over the newborn.

According to Preacher Rowe, Floyd "Fast-Hand" Owens was sentenced to three years in prison, a short sentence compared to most, due to the fact the pastor, James, Ethel, and Grandmother Kay spoke on Floyd's behalf. The men of our church assisted Mrs. Owens with moving her family closer to

Raleigh where her oldest son took a job in a hardware store. She and her oldest daughter became housekeepers at the Hotel Sir Walter. When released from prison, and with a recommendation from Preacher Rowe, Floyd secured a job as a veterinarian assistant. A job he accepted with great enthusiasm. We all understood Floyd was no farmer, and the option of running whiskey was not on the table because Mrs. Owens might kill him.

Jackson removed the bullet from me, and as far as I know, he kept the slug, despite the fact the bullet hole was never repaired. In my opinion, certain scars have great stories behind them.

9

1933: THE NIGHT THE DEVIL CAME TO CHURCH

A light summer breeze flows inside from the open front door and windows when Preacher Rowe concludes a conversation with an elder and steps behind the pulpit to begin the Sunday evening service.

"Good evening, everyone." Now middle-aged, the pastor's waistline has grown about three inches over time. "I'm glad you're all here."

The gentle wind gives me relief by cooling off the sanctuary from the heat of the summer day and by dissolving the sweet smell of perfume mingled with the smell of sweat. Who knew humans could sweat so much? Several folks wave the paper fans advertising This Side of Heaven Funeral Home in front of their faces.

I enjoy the easy time of day once the sun settles, granting enough light I notice the green leaves and pine needles on the tall trees in the graveyard. At times, a refreshing whiff of pine fragrance drifts in through the windows. Pine trees grow as fast as weeds in eastern North Carolina. Mind you, pine trees are a soft wood compared to oak, their branches snap off at the first strong wind. Although, I guess God showed me my own weakness when He split me in half seventy-nine years ago.

A low whistle from outside floats into the sanctuary. The pastor glances toward a window and back to the audience ignoring the noise.

The church building has not changed much since the day in 1899 when I was placed in the sanctuary. Even after thirty-four years, I remain at my eleventh-row position, left side. Although, last week, the sanctuary and the vestibule received a fresh coat of white paint. When the beginnings of a squabble between several ladies disagreeing on the color paint arose, the deacons stepped in and decided the leaders would narrow the paint choices down to two colors for the members vote. White won. I am satisfied with the selection because sunshine pours in through the clear windows and reflects on the walls. I am partial to brightness since my days of standing in the sun.

"Ouch, dang it. Move outta my way, tree." The slurred voice belongs to a man. "I'm gonna ... helpppppp ..."

The voice fades.

"Did you all hear that?" Preacher Rowe's eyes widen.

"Yep," a man says. Others nod.

"Jackson." The pastor finds a young man in the audience. "Please run outside and see if someone's in trouble."

Twenty-year-old Jackson Benjamin Ward, home from college for the summer, does as the preacher asks. From what I hear, Jackson follows in his father's footsteps and will become a lawyer. I wonder if he will defend the likes of Floyd "Fast-Hand" Owens. I recall Jackson appeared way too interested in Mr. Owens.

After a few moments, Jackson returns. "I didn't see anything."

"Okay, take a seat." Preacher Rowe presses a hand against his black tie. "Before I begin tonight's message, one announcement. The funeral for Earl will be here at two o'clock tomorrow. The workers from This Side of Heaven Funeral Home dug the grave yesterday. Pray there's no rain until after the funeral."

I hope the rain stays in the heavens. Since Preacher Rowe shot me, I get the slightest ache around the bullet hole in my seat back when the weather turns nasty, and why no one has repaired me yet, I do not understand. The Wednesday night after I was shot, I overheard a group of boys poking fun at Jackson because his schoolteacher confiscated the bullet. The teacher was none too happy with Jackson bragging about the encounter with Floyd "Fast-Hand" Owens.

"Mildred." The pastor finds her. "Do you have all the food you need to feed Earl's family? With Earl's seven children, grandchildren, and church folks in attendance, I expect a big crowd."

"Yes." She nods. "The ladies auxiliary is furnishing the food."

"Maaa ..." The male voice echoes once more. Several people turn toward the windows facing the graveyard. The preacher's eyes follow the same path.

A girl jumps up and peers out the window. "I still don't see anything." The congregation listens for another sound.

"He ... lp..."

The girl gasps. "I hear the noise again." She turns toward the front. "A ghost, Preacher?"

He chuckles. "No. We don't believe—"

"Help." A sob is heard. "Please."

"Okay, I know we all heard that." Pastor Rowe strides from the pulpit while several people bob their heads.

"John Ashley, Jacob Brown, others of you men please go see what's causing the commotion."

The two stride from the church with Jackson and others

behind them. Jackson should make a good lawyer. With Floyd "Fast-Hand" Owens, he asked many questions. Now, Jackson wants to find out what is happening outside. He has an inquisitive mind, and I wished I could follow the men too.

The pastor and the girl, along with several other children and adults, crowd around and stick their heads out the windows facing the graveyard.

After a few seconds, the girl asks, "What do y'all see?"

"You are kidding me." Jacob chuckles. "John Ashley, you believe this?"

John Ashley's deep laugh rumbles from him. "Is that you, Leonard?"

"Yepppp."

"Seems here, ol' Leonard Gilstrap fell into Earl's grave." Jacob roars with laughter. "Good thing Earl's grave is close by and not one further away from the church, or we wouldn't have heard him."

"Is he okay?" Pastor Rowe leans further out the window.

"Oh yeah, he's okay. Maybe three sheets to the wind though," Jacob says. "What do you have in your hand, Leonard?"

"I got moon ... shine." Leonard slurs. "I need ta go home."

"You need to go to church," John Ashley says.

"Naw ..." Leonard drawls. "Wait. Where ... where did y'all say I was?"

"Earl's grave." Jackson snickers.

"Get me outta here."

John Ashley guffaws. "I guess you better look where you're walking next time."

"See what moonshine will do to you?" Jacob Brown teases.

"Please." Leonard begs. "Get me out."

"Jackson, you jump on down there," Jacob says.

"Here goes." Jackson lands in the hollowed out grave with a loud thud.

I have never seen Leonard Gilstrap but have heard much about him. According to members, he is better known as the town drunk. A great deal of prayer requests have been made on behalf of the man and his elderly mother over the years.

"There's a rope in my truck," another man says before adding, "son, go get it."

"That'll work," John Ashley says.

The next several minutes, laughter reeks from the folks standing at the window and watching the activities. I wish I could see the events unfolding.

"Y'all be ... be care ... ful," Leonard shouts. "I got me a jar here."

"You're in a grave, and all you care about is a jar of 'shine?" Disdain rings from Jacob's voice.

"Leonard, put the Mason jar down," John Ashley demands, "or let Jackson hold your liquor."

"Nope."

"Let go of the jar, Leonard," John Ashley commands.

"You're gonna throw my 'shine out. I paid good money for this here jar."

"Leonard." The name bellows from John Ashley and Jacob at the same time.

"No." Leonard bickers. "I don't wanna."

"If I have to jump in the hole, someone's going to get hurt." John Ashley's voice booms through the windows. "And it ain't going to be me."

Leonard had better listen because John Ashley is six feet, five inches tall, and three-hundred pounds. Nobody scraps with him. Known to the church members as Big John, he is gentle as a teddy bear unless someone, such as Leonard, does not listen to him.

"Uh, okay," Leonard says.

Grumbling from Leonard and grunts from the men assisting him amuse those watching. The moment would have been a sight to see—the town drunk falling into Earl's grave.

"Is he okay?" Pastor Rowe calls out while folks in the church clap and cheer. Too much noise prevents me from hearing the answer. "Let's get to our seats." The preacher straightens then leans back out the window. "Bring Leonard in here. Some preaching is what he needs."

Holding the Mason jar against him, a disgruntled Leonard staggers into the church between Jacob and John Ashley with other fellows following in their wake.

"I don't wanna be here." Leonard stomps a foot and leaves a dirty footprint. All fingers and thumbs, he attempts to tighten the lid on the half empty jar and stumbles against a pew.

"Too bad." Jacob grips Leonard's arm. "He'll sit beside me." The men lead Leonard toward me. "Give me the jar."

"Nope." Leonard's smudged face breaks into a sly grin. "I used my last nickel and bought this here."

"Shameful." Jacob shakes his head. "Your mother could use your help."

Leonard's face sags, he stumbles falling on knees, and drops the jar which rolls a few inches away from him. A few droplets leak from around the lid. Leonard throws an arm up in the air and grabs the jar. "Now look what you made me do."

So, this is Leonard Gilstrap? And the clear liquid is moonshine? The smell is repulsive. How anyone drinks the stuff, I do not know. Reminds me of the whiskey Preacher Rowe and Floyd "Fast-Hand" Owens used when they sterilized their hands before assisting with the birth of Ethel's baby boy.

With the help of the two men, Leonard struggles to a standing position and arches back. Preacher Rowe stares at

Leonard from behind the pulpit with the huge wooden cross hanging on the wall behind him.

"Wrong house." Leonard clasps the half empty jar. "I gotta git home."

Snickers and whisperings resonate throughout the sanctuary. Mothers and fathers shush their children's laughter but to no avail.

Jacob steps into my row and takes a seat on me assuming Leonard will follow suit. John Ashley turns and faces the pew behind me where his wife sits. With no one holding on to him, Leonard does an about face. He attempts an escape. John Ashley whips back around and steps in front of him. Leonard smacks right into John Ashley's broad chest and staggers.

"Ouch."

Jacob reaches from where he sits and grabs hold of Leonard's arm.

"What ..." The befuddled Leonard plops down beside Jacob before he realizes what has happened.

From what I've heard, Leonard is an old pro at drunkenness. Now I realize these stories are true. With greasy hair, dirty and crumpled clothes, Leonard's body reeks from filth, sweat, and moonshine.

"I like my life just the way I am." Leonard jerks forward, but Jacob seizes and secures him to the spot.

At this moment, I understand why Preacher Rowe has declared the evils of moonshine in a great number of his sermons. Thankful for Prohibition, the preacher fears the ban will soon come to an end. According to the pastor, when Franklin Delano Roosevelt won the presidency, he called for Prohibition repeal. If Leonard is an example of what happens when humans overindulge in the homebrew, maybe the moonshine *should* remain outlawed.

Preacher Rowe inhales a deep breath, holds the air for

several seconds, and exhales. "Thanks for joining us tonight, Leonard."

"I don't wanna be here." Leonard's head and jowls shake. Jacob attempts to pull the jar away from him. "Whoa, whoa, whoa. I need dat." Leonard clasps the jar between his palms resembling a hold on a precious piece of porcelain and puts the 'shine between shaky knees.

"Leonard." Preacher Rowe scowls at the man and taps on the pulpit with a knuckle. When more force is needed, the preacher pounds a fist against the wood. Leonard jumps to attention. A few members do as well. "Leonard, God knows you need Him, not the drink. He's brought you here tonight. Now, please respect God and the others. Be quiet, and let's get back to the Word."

"Sorry." Leonard's quietness lasts about ten seconds. "For God loves the world. He gave His Son. Believe in Him. Don't perish but have lasting life."

"Mama, he knows John 3:16." A little girl giggles.

Leonard's reciting the verse amazes me also.

Preacher Rowe stares at Leonard who returns the stare with a faraway look in glassy eyes.

All is quiet, and I wonder how long the silence will last.

"Folks." The preacher scans the crowd. "The Holy Spirit is leading me to change the message I'd plan for tonight. I'm convicted to focus on our guest."

"Preach, Pastor. Preach," a deacon says.

Preacher Rowe points toward the audience. "Every one of you, every person on earth, and every animal on earth knows there is a God in heaven. The birds do not worry how their food is provided, because God takes care of them. God provides rain for the trees and flowers. Satan and the demons know God exists and what's in store for them."

Jacob slides a look at Leonard who gazes forward.

"Do you know what our Heavenly Father did for us?" the pastor asks.

"Yep." Leonard fidgets with the jar. "His Son died for us."

The pastor studies Leonard. "That's right. Jesus was born, crucified, and resurrected that we might have life. No one comes to the Father except through Jesus Christ." A more charismatic lady raises her hand, waves side to side, and lowers her arm.

Several pairs of eyes observe Leonard. Despite an unpromising entrance, I would say Leonard's behavior, although he fiddles with the jar and bounces a leg nonstop, has been pretty decent. Jacob grips Leonard's upper arm and shoulder holding on tighter, wedging him into my corner.

With a grunt and a sharp twist of his upper body, Leonard's shoulder breaks from Jacob's grip. He bolts upward, hitting the woman before him in the back of the head. The jar crashes on the floor at the right angle and shatters.

"No." Leonard leaps into the aisle. Jacob grabs for him and misses. John Ashley reaches out. The squirrely Leonard is too fast for the big man.

Folks' mouths stand agape. Leonard skedaddles down the aisle toward the exit. At the open front door, he stumbles over the threshold. "Daggummit." Leonard grabs the doorframe, steadies himself, and scampers from the church.

"Jacob, John Ashley, please get him," Preacher Rowe's face grows red. "If the devil wants to come to church, by God's power and our men's strength, he's going to stay here until I'm finished."

Folks lurch near the edge of their seats and turn toward the front door. Others stand in the aisle waiting for what will happen next. Preacher Rowe's eyes focus on the open door. His hands grip the pulpit, his knuckles turning white.

"You can't make me go back inside." Leonard's shouts echo through the open doorway. "I ain't going."

"Is that right?" John Ashley's voice booms again.

"Yep."

I hear a scuffle.

Whack.

"Did he hit me with a puny fist, Jacob?"

"Sure did, Big John."

"Is that all you got? I didn't feel a thing." A moment of silence before John Ashley's voice rumbles. "The next time you take a swing at someone my size, remember the consequences. Most guys swing back. Good thing I'm a nice guy."

"Sure is," Jacob says.

"Now," John Ashley demands, "get in the church."

Leonard protests. "I ain't going back inside."

A few minutes later, the crowd shuffles backward to their seats when Jacob and John Ashley drag an irate Leonard into the church. The two gentlemen interlock arms with Leonard, one on each side of him. Escorting Leonard back to me, the men sit with him wedged between them. John Ashley's big foot pushes the broken glass under the pew in front of him. The smell is as sharp as the paint thinner used in here last week.

"I don't wanna be here." Leonard blubbers like a baby.

"Too bad." Preacher Rowe wipes a sweaty brow with a handkerchief. "Be quiet. The more you interrupt, the longer I'll preach."

Leonard burps and waves a hand at the pastor. "I'll shut up then. Get the preachin' over with." Leonard projects a loud whisper in Jacob's direction, but everyone hears him. "My mama's gonna be proud I come to church tonight."

Preacher Rowe pauses and bows his head. I assume he utters a prayer for strength to get through tonight. The pastor looks up and continues with his voice lowering to normal, and repeating John 3:16. After gazing around at the entire congregation, he reads the new commandment Jesus gave in John, "...That ye love one another; as I have loved you, that ye also love one another."

A few heads spin in Leonard's direction.

"If we show Christian love to the poor, the homeless, the needy, the lost, what better testimony are we for God? God loves them as much as he loves us. Family and friends will let us down. God ... He," the preacher points heavenward, "will not let us down. God's love is everlasting. And those God loves, He also disciplines."

Preacher Rowe stares at Leonard for an unusual length of time. "You children will relate to this, and I'm sure you adults will recall what happened when you misbehaved. When my brother and I were in trouble with our mother, she demanded we head outside and break off a long stem from our mulberry bush. Then, we'd lug the switch inside for her." The pastor chuckles. "Before she used the stick on our backsides, she'd explain how much she loved us, and because she loved us, we were getting spanked."

"Uh-huh," someone remarks. Leonard keeps quiet.

The preacher closes his Bible. "My point, 'For whom the Lord loveth he correcteth; even as a father the son in whom he delighteth.' Proverbs chapter three, verse twelve."

Preacher Rowe steps down the three altar steps and in front of the pulpit, Bible in hand and with head bent. I assume he is praying. Ladies stop fanning themselves. Children look up. Men sit straighter. The congregation focuses on the pastor. The only sound is from outside—crickets chirping. And Leonard, he does not move a muscle.

Preacher Rowe lifts his head and looks at the pianist who strides to the piano, and with light fingers, touches the beginning chords of "Just As I Am." While she plays, the pastor watches Leonard.

"If you want to experience love, peace, and contentment." He holds up an index finger. "Love which will help you face anything this earth has to offer, there's one way."

Now, all is silent, and time appears to stand still. Then, only as the Holy Spirit works in someone's life, the drunken stupor vanishes from Leonard. He rises. "How?" The question comes husky and thick.

The preacher points toward the cross on the wall. "Believe on the Lord Jesus Christ, and you shall be saved."

Tears fill Leonard's eyes and stream down his grimy face. Leonard's entire body trembles. "I do. I wanna, preacher. I do. I wanna believe He could love someone like me."

The preacher walks and stops next to my pew. John Ashley moves out of the way. The preacher reaches in, pulls Leonard toward him, and escorts him to the altar. Jacob, John Ashley, and deacons from the four corners of the church follow. Preacher Rowe and Leonard kneel at the altar with others surrounding them. The pianist continues playing, and a few people hum. The working power of God surrounds us all tonight.

The preacher finishes praying with Leonard. "Amen." He, Leonard, and the others stand and face the congregation. Leonard swipes tears from red eyes. The preacher grabs him in a sideways bear hug. "Welcome to the family of Christ, Leonard."

"Thanks." Leonard sniffles.

Preacher Rowe gestures to members. They come forward and welcome Leonard as a new believer in Christ. An older lady wipes his cheeks with her handkerchief. Men grasp Leonard's hand in a hearty handshake. The ladies are more reserved. One little girl hugs Leonard, and an older couple invites him to their home next Sunday after the service for lunch.

After the last person shakes Leonard's hand, the pastor gives the benediction, and folks meander out of the church.

With everyone gone, I have a clear view of the preacher and Leonard standing alone in the vestibule. Preacher Rowe claps Leonard's shoulder. "There's a bucket and mop in the closet. Pull the door shut when you've finished mopping up all the moonshine."

"Huh?" Leonard frowns.

"Been smelling your moonshine all night since you dropped the jar. Time to clean the stink from our church."

"Oh, yessir." Leonard wipes a hand over a scruffy chin. "I'll get da floor real clean, preacher."

"Good." Preacher Rowe beams and adds before leaving, "Try not to fall back into Earl's grave on your way home."

Leonard grins. "I hear you, preacher. Don't want dat to happen again."

Pastor Rowe departs, leaving Leonard and me.

Leonard retrieves the bucket and mop. He gets to work, all the while talking with God in a backwoods way. "Thank you, Jesus." Leonard picks up the broken jar pieces and mops the moonshine from the floor. "I don't need no more of da stuff."

By the time he finishes, the floor shines brighter than I had seen in years. Wrapped up in a talk with God, Leonard mopped a few areas twice, and believe me, he and God had an enormous amount to discuss.

Not a typical Sunday evening when the devil comes to church with boldness as he did tonight. Leonard enters full of the devil, but by the grace of God, leaves full of the Holy Spirit.

The next Sunday morning, Leonard arrives showered and shaved with hair slicked back. He sports a navy suit and carries an old Bible. On Leonard's right arm, he smiles down at Mrs.

Gilstrap, his mother, and guides her to a seat on me. People stare and in an instant, recover welcoming mother and son to church. Pastor Rowe stops by and shakes their hands.

Last Sunday night, the Holy Spirit worked a miracle in Leonard's life. Now, the congregation and I watch while he serves his Lord and Savior. And, his mama.

10

1949: A PIG NAMED BAR-B-QUE

*P*astor Dunn, who has been with us for three years, stands behind the pulpit. "Ladies, I saw all the food you prepared for our annual picnic. Those tables under the pavilion are loaded with vittles. Smells some kind of good. That small slice of ham Mrs. Craig snuck me ..." Pastor Dunn smacks his lips. "Let's say, my sermon might get cut short this morning."

Mrs. Craig blushes at the pastor's compliment. Whenever a food related function takes place at the church, she gets accolades galore. I overheard one man say her pineapple glazed ham is "to die for," which seems extreme to me.

Folks are in better spirits this year than in the past few. In the 1930s, the Great Depression hit America, and a large handful in our rural area lost their homes and farms. With children experiencing malnourishment, families did what they could to survive. Pumpkin Creek members shared what the Lord had given them and offered two soup meals a week to the community, under the pavilion.

Before the full rebound from the Great Depression, the

United States entered World War II. I will never forget December 7, 1941, the day the Japanese attacked Pearl Harbor. The next day, the US declared war on Japan while on December 11, 1941, Adolf Hitler declared war on America. The days following, Pastor Dunn and the elders ushered families and friends into the sanctuary who prayed over our country.

With our men at war, women stepped up and worked jobs the men had held before leaving to fight. I recall Mrs. Sarah Ward, a lady who encouraged progress. She was the first lady in our congregation to drive an automobile and had electricity installed throughout her home when power came to our rural area. Sarah never lived to see the array of changes for women I hear about or see from our members—updated appliances in the kitchen, more job opportunities outside the home, and shorter dresses. I think she would have loved the television which is becoming more popular in family life.

Our members have felt, seen, and lived destruction over the past two decades. However, the Pumpkin Creek United Church members have followed the Word and persevered. Each year's picnic is a celebration of what the Lord has done at the church and within the community.

After the opening prayer, weekly announcements, a hymn, and offering, the choir belts out a special song. Pastor Dunn prays and opens his Bible. He reads a passage of Scripture and preaches. When I hear several folks snap shut their Bibles, I suppose the pastor is almost finished with the sermon, but Pastor Dunn flips to another chapter and reads. The sermon lasts another fifteen minutes. I see from the way the Craig children squirm on my pew, they wished he would let them head toward the food.

"Okay folks, I'm going to finish up." Pastor Dunn walks

from behind the pulpit, steps down, and stands beside the altar table facing the crowd.

The church interior remains the same, not much money for updates, although I have heard suggestions of indoor plumbing and carpet. I remain in the same place—eleventh row, left side.

When the pianist strikes the chords for "Just As I Am," Wiley and Ronnie Sanders rush forward with tears streaming down their faces. The brothers, two of the most rambunctious and mischievous little boys I have ever seen in here, have hearts of gold. The pastor watches as Mr. and Mrs. Sanders make a beeline to their boys. The Sanders live on a pig farm belonging to their family for three generations. By God's grace, the farm has survived over the decades.

Wiley and Ronnie have slipped critters into the sanctuary in the past—a puppy, kitten, and a lizard. The lizard escaped during one sermon and, to this day, no one has forgotten the commotion the creature caused among the womenfolk. I have not forgotten either. Two ladies stood on me stamping their heels against my seat. The lizard was never found, and if female screams could kill, the poor lizard died that day in the church.

I feel certain they received a spanking on the Sunday of the lizard. Mr. Sanders had Wiley's arm in a tight grip when they left the church with Mrs. Sanders following on her husband's heels and gripping Ronnie by the ear. Before the family exited the church, Mr. Sanders gritted his teeth and said, "Wait until I get you boys outside."

Kneeling on the lower altar step now, the boys' cries and voices penetrate throughout the church and blend in with the music. Pastor Dunn crouches between them and places an arm around each of their shoulders. Mrs. Sanders sits on an altar step and rubs Ronnie's back. Mr. Sanders kneels on the other side of Wiley.

At the song's conclusion, Pastor Dunn and the entire Sanders family stand. He waves a hand, and silence falls over the congregation. "Folks, please be seated," the pastor says. "We have a problem. Bar-B-Que is missing."

Yes, the boys have a pet pig named Bar-B-Que. Ironic, right? North Carolina barbeque—shredded pork as those outside of the south refer to the meat—fried pork chops, baked hams, sausage, and pickled pigs' feet are staples in the area. When these farmers and their wives talk about an upcoming pig slaughter, the announcement is made in church weeks prior, and volunteers come out of the woodwork to help. I hear every part of the pig is used for food—which does not sound appetizing to me.

A young girl exclaims, "Oh, no."

"What happened?" A man near the front asks.

"We're hoping to find out," Mr. Sanders says.

Six months ago, Mr. Sanders gave the boys the runt of the litter when a sow birthed piglets. Wrapped in a blanket, the brothers slipped Bar-B-Que into the church, sat on me, and nestled the pig between them. Their parents sang in the choir. Mr. and Mrs. Sanders were as surprised as the rest of the churchgoers when everyone heard the first *oink*. With a red face, Mr. Sanders marched toward Wiley and Ronnie. But Pastor Dunn grinned and waved him back to the choir.

Wiley and Ronnie walked the aisle that day wanting Bar-B-Que dedicated to the Lord. Youngsters have such innocent hearts compared to old fogeys. The good-natured pastor prayed over Bar-B-Que, thanking God for their pet and praying for the pig's safety. After he finished the benediction, Ronnie asked the preacher if he and Wiley could stand in the vestibule with the pastor while he said goodbye to members when they left the church. Pastor Dunn suggested Bar-B-Que needed more wiggle room to stretch after being snuggled in the blanket. He hinted the boys should take Bar-B-Que outside where everyone could get a good look at him. The boys raced down the aisle with their pet pig bouncing in Wiley's arms. Their care for the piglet was adorable.

The boys continued bringing Bar-B-Que inside the sanctuary until the oinks became too frequent. Before anyone could say amen in agreement with the pastor's preaching, Bar-B-Que would oink which caused laughter instead of meditation on the Word. Pastor Dunn proposed bringing Bar-B-Que to church and tying him to a bush during the service. Afterward, the children could pet and play with the pig.

Today, Pastor Dunn walks forward. He surveys the crowd. "Times are hard folks. Since we're a tightknit community, if any of you know the whereabouts of Bar-B-Que, please let Mr. Sanders or me know."

Ronnie clenches both fists. "He was stolen." Mrs. Sanders pulls him close by her side.

"Ronnie," Pastor Dunn glances at him, "we don't know for sure."

"How 'bout those boot prints around da pig pen," Wiley blurts. "They don't belong to me, Ronnie, Pa, or Leonard. They were huge prints. Pa's feet ain't that big."

"I'm not sure what's happened, Preacher." Mr. Sanders rakes a hand through his hair. "I've got wind of someone trespassing around my place." He finds a man in his late forties. "Right, Leonard?"

Leonard Gilstrap locks eyes with Mr. Sanders. "Dat's right."

Since the night he fell into Earl's grave sixteen years ago, Leonard has remained a devout Christian. Mrs. Gilstrap passed away in the spring of 1941, and Preacher Rowe presided over her funeral. Two days later the preacher went home with the Lord too. Soon after, God sent a newly wedded Pastor Dunn, who could not serve in the war because of asthma. The Lord blessed us with a new pastor and Leonard with a job as a farmhand on the Sanders farm.

"Me and the boys lock dat pig gate every night." Leonard glances around.

With vigor, Wiley and Ronnie nod their heads.

"So, I's decided." Leonard stands. "I's gonna spend the night under the shelter. See if I could catch whose been snoopin' round. I did find this in the pig muck." From an oversized pocket, he pulls a worn gray, flat cap. Leonard waves the hat around. A silver fishhook pinned on the side glistens. "Cleaned the hat, best I could."

Mrs. Wilbur Craig shrieks.

Ellie Craig twists and faces her father. "Pa, ain't the cap yours?"

Concerned expressions fill the churchgoer's faces. Everyone's eyes turn the way of Mr. Craig who sits in the corner of me closest to the aisle.

A deep crease forms on Mr. Sanders forehead. "Is it, Wilbur?"

Ronnie cries out. "Please give Bar-B-Que back to us."

"We raised 'im since he was a baby." Wiley wipes his tear-streaked face. "We love him and miss him."

"The past year ..." With slumped shoulders, Wilbur Craig's husky voice sounds full of discouragement. "The past year has been hard on me and my family. We lost the farm to the bank."

With farmers in financial trouble, prayer meetings about the economy, crops, and foreclosures have taken place. From what I hear, times are changing for the better, however the change has not arrived in our neck of the woods. Several times the offering was miniscule, Pastor Dunn barely received a decent wage in his weekly paycheck. The congregation rounded up items—vegetables, eggs, a chicken, or firewood—to assist the pastor's family through those hard times.

"Where is he?' Wiley wanders toward Wilbur. Ronnie, their parents, and the pastor follow. They form a semicircle in the aisle near Wilbur.

"I, um ..." Wilbur stammers, "I ... uh ..."

Mr. Sanders and Pastor Dunn glance at each other. By the look on their faces, I assume they suspect Bar-B-Que has met an unfortunate fate.

Mrs. Craig hollers at her husband. "Wilbur Xavier Craig."

Ellie's voice trembles. "Pa, you didn't." Her younger brothers and sisters stare wide-eyed at their pa.

Mrs. Craig jerks up from her seat. "I thought you were in the next town over working. Were you up to no good over at Curtis's shack preparing a stolen pig? No wonder all you brought home was pork and not a paycheck. You lied. You ain't got a job, have you?"

Wilbur's face and neck turn bright red. He stares at the floor.

Mrs. Craig throws her hands up in disgust, a tight grimace on her lips.

"Uh-oh," someone says.

"Excuse me, Mr. Sanders, Wiley, Ronnie," the pastor says. The youngsters pivot with their eyes hopeful. "Remember last Sunday's sermon about forgiveness?"

Ronnie nods. Wiley shrugs. "Not all of it."

Pastor Dunn places a hand on each boy's shoulders. "Jesus died for your sins. Every time you sin, what does Jesus do when you ask?"

"Forgives me." Wiley glances downward. "Cause yesterday I took a piece of Ronnie's chocolate candy."

Ronnie darts bulging eyes toward Wiley. "Meany."

"Boys, listen," Mr. Sanders says.

The pastor glances at Wilbur and the boys. "Wilbur has done something—"

"And I'm not proud of my actions." Wilbur wipes a hand over his mouth. "I can't find work, and my kids are hungry."

"I'm gonna be sick." Mrs. Craig plops down and fans her cheeks.

Mr. Craig's face sags. "There's been a few days where we didn't have anything to feed the kids."

Wiley murmurs, "You *ate* Bar-B-Que?"

Ronnie's face crumples, and Mr. Sanders scoops him up.

"I'm sorry. We were hungry." Wilbur pleads and begs. "Please, please forgive me." Wilbur looks at Mr. Sanders. "I didn't mean to grab Bar-B-Que. I couldn't see, nighttime and all. I'm sorry."

Mr. Sanders frowns. "Still, you stole from us."

Wilbur nods. "I'll do anything to pay off my debt to you." He slips off me, kneels before Wiley, and grabs the boy's shoulders. "I'm sorry, Wiley. Please, y'all find forgiveness in your hearts toward me?"

No one moves an inch or says a word. Everyone waits.

Wiley tilts his head and watches the man pleading before him. Wilbur releases the boy. Wiley glances around at the people watching and waiting for an answer. He focuses on his pa and turns back facing Wilbur. "If y'all need food, why didn't y'all come see my pa?"

"I don't know." Wilbur hesitates. "I was ashamed. I couldn't feed my kids."

Ronnie cries. "I want Bar-B-Que."

"Ronnie." Mr. Sanders frowns. "We've had lots of animals come and go. Bar-B-Que is gone. Now, I've explained the circle of life regarding your pets before. Remember?" Ronnie wipes a runny nose with a forearm.

Wiley clutches the older man's shoulders, and they are face

to face with each other. "I'll forgive ya because that's what Jesus would do."

"You will?" Ronnie wiggles, and Mr. Sanders places him down beside Wiley. "Then, me too." Ronnie scrunches his nose. "But I don't wanna."

"And I ain't happy bout ya eatin' my pig," Wiley says.

Ronnie points a finger at Wilbur. "Me either."

Mr. Sanders places a hand on each of his son's shoulders. "I'm proud of you, boys."

"Me too." Pastor Dunn looks at the brothers. Two elders echo the affirmation.

"Thank you." Wilbur grabs Wiley and hugs him. "I'm sorry. I shouldn't have stolen your pig." After releasing Wiley, Wilbur sniffles and with a calloused hand, wipes tears from his eyes.

Wilbur stands, and Pastor Dunn pats him on the back. Mrs. Craig and her children remain seated on me, disappointment written on their faces. Folks gather closer around Wilbur and the boys, and they applaud them on their Christian actions toward each other. As expected, Wiley and Ronnie receive most of the praise. Wilbur receives hard stares and shakes of the head.

"Boys, I have good news." Mr. Sanders looks at Wiley and Ronnie. "Another sow is having piglets."

Wiley grins. "Can we have the runt again?"

Mr. Sanders nods.

"Yippee," the boys shout, jumping up and down.

Pastor Dunn places both hands on his hips. "See how God works all things for good to glorify His name?"

"Guess what I'm gonna name him." Ronnie grins and exposes a gap where he lost a front tooth. "Bacon." He arches back, pokes out his stomach, and rubs in circular motions across his shirt. "Cause I loooove bacon."

Giggles and laughter spring forth in the church. Mr. Sanders ruffles Ronnie's hair. There is never a dull moment with Wiley and Ronnie Sanders around.

"Me too, Ronnie. Me too." Pastor Dunn gestures for the crowd to follow him. "Let's head out and enjoy the picnic."

"Yeah, I'm hungry." Ronnie pushes through the crowd and races from the church with others straggling behind.

At the back of the crowd, two older women chitchat when the plump one halts by me. The tall, thin woman turns around with puzzlement in her eyes, waiting.

The plumb lady places a thick hand on my back. "Do you think?" She giggles and shakes her head. "No." She gazes open-mouthed at her friend. "Mrs. Craig's ham used to be ..."

"Oh my." The tall lady slaps a gloved hand over her mouth then regains composure. "Today's picnic will be one where her pineapple glazed ham used to have a name."

"Poor, Mrs. Craig."

"Don't you mean poor Bar-B-Que?"

After the incident, all returned to normal at Pumpkin Creek United Church. Mr. Craig worked off his debt to Mr. Sanders, and the Sanders family made sure the Craig family never went without food again. And rumor spread amongst the members, Mrs. Craig never brought another ham to a church picnic.

11

1955: GOD KNOWS WHAT'S UNDER YOUR HAT AND IN YOUR HEART

On this glorious Easter morning, Ida Belle Baker sashays into church wearing a white dress with royal blue trim and a huge royal blue hat with a long, gray feather protruding from the back panel. A white ribbon wraps around the wide brim. The feather appears to sprout from her head, and the hat catches the eye of most everyone when she proceeds down the church aisle. The headpiece resembles a lampshade Pastor Dunn's wife purchased and brought in one day to show him while he practiced a sermon.

Funny, I did not realize hats were shaped with a likeness to lampshades, but I see they are.

Folks stare open-mouthed at the unusual headpiece. By far, the ugliest hat in the church.

"Bless her heart," a middle-aged lady says to her husband when Ida Belle walks past them. I have heard the phrase tons of times amongst the women in the church, and I do believe the words suggest an insult, in a nice way to lessen the blow.

Ida Belle is not what most folks call an attractive woman. Besides the humongous hat, her nose is too big for her face.

When she squints, her beady, brown eyes hide behind the bright, blue eyeshadow she always wears. Ida Belle's dress hangs on her oversized waist and hips, not in a flattering way. Stockings cover her large legs and are held up by Baby Doll pumps, white, of course, matching her dress although much of her foot fat spills over the shoes sides. I pray those heels do not collapse with her standing on them.

Understand, I am not gossiping about Ida Belle. I state the facts as I observe them. And, she does have a tendency to speak unkind words about others. Therefore, I do believe "the abundance of the heart his mouth speaketh." You know, she is not a nice person.

Truth be told, she has a cousin named Maybelle, the two resemble twins in appearance but not in personality. Maybelle is kind-spirited and generous in all she does to serve the Lord and is liked by the church members. Ida Belle is not. To make matters worse, both women are in pursuit of a husband, therefore, the competition is on between them.

Maybelle is the librarian at the elementary school. Once the Pentecostal church went belly-up, she moved her membership to our church. When the cousins inherited their aunt's small house on the edge of town, Ida Belle moved up from Georgia and now works the drugstore lunch counter. Since she already had a home, Maybelle sold her half to her cousin. Rumor is, Ida Belle did not want to pay her fair share and implied the house had flaws—a damaged roof, rusting pipes, and termites.

I hate termites.

Maybelle's attorney, Jackson Benjamin Ward, ensured she received her fair share from the sale.

I still wonder if Jackson's schoolteacher ever returned the bullet Jackson pulled from me.

Across from me, Ida Belle squeezes into the eleventh row

from the front on the right side of the aisle. Her face breaks into a huge smile when she looks my way and notices the back of the head of the man that she has her eye upon—Darryl Dunn, the pastor's single, war veteran brother. Darryl visits on Christmas and Easter, and other times throughout the year. Today, Darryl sits on the pew in front of me.

After the opening prayer and announcements, Pastor Dunn lifts his hymnal. "Turn to page 162 and let's sing 'He is Risen.'" The congregation stands. When the pianist strikes the beginning notes, the pastor moves a hand and conducts the song's words.

"I'm plenty late." A frazzled Maybelle exhales. She rushes down the aisle and stops beside me, positioning her Easter hat on her head. Uh-oh, her hat and dress identical to Ida Belle's.

The folks at Pumpkin Creek United Church take pride in their Easter outfits. The 1940s were tough on folks, and now the economy is on an upward trend, folks have more money to spend on things. I see women are buying more fancy clothes, hats, and accessories. Since the men have returned from the Korean War and reunited with their families, hope shines on their faces and in their attitudes.

I must say, on Easter, all the folks look right spiffy in their bright, spring-colored attire. With new fashion styles every year, the ladies buy modern hats. I am not surprised the hat fashion of Ida Belle and Maybelle is big and gaudy compared with the other ladies in the church.

I notice all available ladies of marriage age are dressed up. I wonder if the reason is the Easter celebration or to impress Darryl Dunn. One mother said he resembled a singer named Elvis Presley whom she called "gorgeous."

"Excuse me." Maybelle, fanning her face with a white-gloved hand, steps into my row behind Darryl. A couple slides over accommodating her. Positioned at the edge of their rows, the cousins are across the aisle from each other.

Darryl, glancing across his shoulder toward Maybelle, smiles, and she blushes. Ida Belle glances over at the movement and whips her head back around in a double-take fumbling with her hymnal. Ida Belle stops singing and hisses. She utters loud enough for those nearby to hear, "Maybelle, your outfit."

Maybelle twists toward her cousin. Her jaw drops. She peruses Ida Belle from hat to shoe.

I empathize with Maybelle because she always tries to do what is right in God's eyes. She delivers library books to the elderly, tutors children who have difficulty reading, and attends the ladies' Bible study—even if she is always late.

Ida Belle, on the other hand, looks after Ida Belle and has the audacity to ask favors from Maybelle and others when she is capable of doing things herself. Among the gossipers, their description of Ida Belle is that she is selfish. Since Maybelle is a sincere person and respected in the community, I believe Ida Belle is jealous of her. Nevertheless, neither lady has ever married and today, I do not envy Darryl Dunn because the cousins and other single ladies have set their sights on him.

Dear Lord, watch over the man.

Now, where they found two identical royal blue hats with feathers is beyond my depth of knowledge.

Ida Belle points a stiff finger at Maybelle's dress.

Maybelle mouths, "What?" A seething Ida Belle twists her head back toward the front, and Maybelle shrugs. She faces forward too.

The song ends. "Please be seated." Pastor Dunn places the hymnal down and picks up his Bible. He reads a verse about tithes and offerings. "Will the ushers come forward for our offering?"

Four men, scattered about the filled sanctuary, rise. One

of whom is Darryl. The men walk forward and stop in front of the altar table where four, gold-plated offering plates rest. One usher picks up the plates and hands them out to the others.

"I'm pleased my brother is visiting with us. Our family has enjoyed our time with him. Darryl, would you please pray?" Pastor Dunn and the congregation bow their heads.

Before Darryl says a word, a loud whisper erupts from Ida Belle's mouth. "I can't believe you."

With head bent and eyes closed, Pastor Dunn pops one eye open and peers at the cause of the disturbance. One usher looks over his shoulder and scowls.

Maybelle holds a finger at her lips. "Shhh." Both women bow their heads and close their eyes.

"Lord, thank You for a wonderful Easter day and the resurrection of Your Son, Jesus Christ. Help us do Your will and give according to what You have given us. Let us use the offering to glorify Your Name. In Jesus's name, amen."

"Amen," the pastor and the other ushers say in unison. The pianist plays, "The Old Rugged Cross." The ushers start at the front pews and pass the offering plates down each row working their way to the last row.

With bulging eyes, Ida Belle glares at Maybelle. "You shopped at Laura's Dress Shop." Two folks seated on Ida Belle's pew, frown at her. When Darryl stops and hands the offering plate to Ida Belle, she closes her mouth and turns google-eyed. After the ushers pass her, Ida Belle turns toward Maybelle again.

Maybelle tilts her head toward Ida Belle and says in a loud whisper, "Yep, I went to Laura's." No big surprise, Laura's Dress Shop is located in the next town over and provides clothes for the hard-to-fit woman. I guess the shop provides hats too. "You said you were going to Raleigh to find"—she makes quotation marks with her hands, "'the perfect Easter dress.'" Maybelle grimaces. "Now, be quiet."

Ida Belle's face turns red. "Don't tell me what to do."

Maybelle throws a hard glare back at Ida Belle. "You should've shown me your Easter outfit when I asked you. You shouldn't have hidden the dress and hat from me. Now look at us."

Ida Belle's face twists. Her voice carries over the soft music. "Go to the ladies' room and remove your hat." Folks on the surrounding pews toss a glance her way. Pastor Dunn looks up from his notes.

A year back, restrooms, one for the men and another for the women, were added in the front taking up square footage from the vestibule. The addition made life easier for mothers when their little ones needed a restroom.

"I will not." Maybelle faces front. Ida Belle huffs.

When the ushers finish, they wait near the back row. The music continues, and the congregation faces forward. Pastor Dunn nods, and the ushers walk down the aisle toward the altar table.

When the ushers step near Ida Belle, she throws her purse into the youngest usher's path. "Oops." Ida Belle feigns. She stands, steps into the aisle, and retrieves the pocketbook smacking her enormous hip into him.

The usher stumbles, smashes into Darryl on his left who in turn knocks into Maybelle's shoulder and head. Coins and bills drop to the floor. Maybelle's hat follows suit. A cheeky smile pulls at Ida Belle's mouth.

"Yikes." Maybelle rises grabbing at her hat.

Folks gasp, and the preacher frowns.

To steady Maybelle, Darryl grasps her elbow. "I'm sorry, ma'am." On hands and knees, the youngest usher picks up the money and places the cash into a plate held for him by an older usher.

Ida Belle stares at Darryl touching Maybelle's arm. Anger rips across her face.

Maybelle bats her lashes. "That's okay." Darryl releases her arm. Before the young usher picks up Maybelle's hat, Ida Belle glares at the hat, looks at Maybelle, and the hat again.

Maybelle's eyes look as if they will pop out of her head. She exclaims, "No."

The youngest usher snatches his hand back when he sees Ida Belle lift her thick foot. With her heel, she stamps down and crushes the hat. The feather on the hat breaks in half. The young usher stares wide-eyed.

With disapproval creasing the oldest usher's brow, he reaches down, grabs the hat, and hands the rumpled mess to Maybelle. "You should be ashamed of yourself, Ida Belle Baker." Ida Belle cuts her eyes at the usher and shrugs.

Two children point at Maybelle's destroyed hat. A lady slaps her hand over her mouth.

"Ladies." Pastor Dunn's voice rises over the soft music. "What's going on?"

What a ruckus Ida Belle started. And, on Easter Sunday.

Maybelle ignores the pastor. "Look at what you did." She fluffs the damaged hat and places the ill-balanced piece on her head. "Your behavior is not becoming of a Christian." Ida Belle snorts and turns away from her cousin. Pastor Dunn glares at Ida Belle.

With the money back in the offering plates, Darryl nudges an usher. The men stand erect ready to finish the walk down the aisle. Before the men walk two steps, Ida Belle lashes out at Maybelle. "You always screw things up, you dimwit."

Pastor Dunn holds up a hand. The pianist stops playing. All eyes are on the cousins and ushers. Pity flashes in

Maybelle's eyes. "Me, a dimwit. You don't stand a chance with him."

"You don't either." Ida Belle snaps back.

"Who?" Pastor Dunn demands. "What's wrong with you two?"

Ida Belle and Maybelle fire a quick look at Darryl.

Bright red stains Darryl's cheeks. "Me?"

Before Maybelle realizes what her cousin is up to, Ida Belle rears back and lands a right hook into Maybelle's nose. Maybelle staggers back.

The congregation stares, and several mouths hang open.

"Ouch." Maybelle grabs her nose and tears hit her eyes. Drops of blood drip from her nose, staining her gloves. "You're hateful." Maybelle grips Ida Belle's hat and yanks. "I'll show him the true you." Ida Belle's blonde wig and hat rip from her head, the artificial hair hanging from the hat in Maybelle's hand.

I guess Maybelle is tired of being nice to her selfish and rude cousin.

When a small boy points, everyone else gasps and stares.

Rage spews from Ida Belle's mouth. "Maybelle Baker." She clasps her stocking covered head.

Pastor Dunn shouts, "Darryl. Men. Separate those ladies." Darryl and the young usher hand their plates to the older ushers.

The men close in at the moment Ida Belle draws back her fist again, punches forward missing Maybelle and knocks the youngest usher in the eye. He stumbles back holding the left side of his face. The women circle each other.

Maybelle demands, "Why do you always act this way? You're ruining Easter. Now, sit down, or we'll get thrown out of church."

"I don't care. He's mine." Ida Belle's eyes blaze. "I had my eye on him first. Now look at what you've done."

"Me?" With her free hand, Maybelle points an index finger. "You're crazy. No man wants you."

"Oh, yeah. Look who's talking." Ida Belle slaps at Maybelle's head, pushing the hat lop-sided on her head. "You're naive. No man wants you either."

Maybelle throws the wig and hat onto the floor, raises her bloodied gloved fingers, stares at the front of Ida Belle's white dress, and flashes a wicked smile.

Ida Bella yells, "Don't you dare."

Maybelle swipes her hand across Ida Belle's chest. She stares at her handiwork. Ida Belle peers down at the red streak. Maybelle's mouth tilts upward at the corners. "A scarlet letter, like in the book."

Pastor Dunn smacks the pulpit with a palm. "Ladies, behave."

"You ... you ..." Ida Belle spits out her words. "No man wants a stupid cow like you."

Maybelle growls. "You couldn't keep a man if your life depended on it."

Three times, Pastor Dunn pounds a fist against the pulpit. "Pull those women apart."

Darryl jumps smack dab between the two women. The cousins stop all movement. They stare at him.

"She started everything." Ida Belle stamps her foot. "She has on my hat and dress." Her face wilts. "You knew I wanted to impress Darryl."

Darryl tilts his head. "Why are you ladies trying to impress me?"

"You're single." A deep crease forms between Ida Belle's brows. "Look around. There's single women everywhere."

Darryl glances over the crowd and in swift movements,

single ladies turn away. None want to get caught watching the bachelor.

The situation is amusing. However, I do feel sorry for the Baker cousins with all the competition sitting in our church.

"You impressed me all right." Darryl chuckles looking at Ida Belle. "The way you throw a punch. Maybe you should've served in the war."

Ida Belle grins at the compliment. Maybelle looks downward.

"Ladies, what you wear doesn't matter." Darryl glances between the cousins. Maybelle and Ida Belle focus on the bachelor. "You know why? Because God knows what's under your hat and in your heart. And fighting is no way to get a husband." Maybelle's bottom lip quivers. Ida Belle's cheeks turn bright red. Darryl looks over the congregation. "Good thing I'm heading out tomorrow."

Ida Belle exclaims, "What?"

"I'm already taken. I'm moving to Florida where my fiancée and her family live. I have a job lined up down there."

At the other end of my row, a disappointed mother of a young, single lady sighs. "Ohhh."

Ida Belle scrunches her face in defeat. "You have a fiancée?"

Maybelle's shoulders sag. She whines. "We'll never get married."

Ida Belle spots her hat and wig on the floor, twists around, and grabs her head with both hands. She looks at Maybelle. Soft chuckles erupt from among the crowd. Hatless and wigless, she dashes from the church.

Maybelle puts her hand over her mouth and glances over the congregation. "Sorry, Pastor Dunn. Sorry, everyone." She gathers her purse, Ida Belle's pocketbook, and the hat with the wig still attached. She follows her cousin.

Sitting on the pew behind me, twelve-year old Ronnie Sanders blurts to his older brother, Wiley, "Those two were hilarious."

Wiley grins. "Best fight I've seen in a while."

Mrs. Sanders grabs Ronnie's ear and twists. "Be quiet." She looks at her husband who attempts keeping his laughter in check. She releases her son's ear, shakes her head, and chuckles along with everyone else in the church.

Openmouthed, Pastor Dunn stares at the front door, where the Baker cousins exited a second ago.

I never saw Ida Belle or Maybelle again. A widowed pastor with a young daughter was hired as the preacher at the Baptist church in the next town over. I heard Ida Belle and Maybelle rushed to the pastor's doorstep and welcomed him to the area.

The ladies of Pumpkin Creek United Church wished Ida Belle and Maybelle their best.

Bless their hearts.

12

1967: CORNED BEEF HASH

For the first time ever, carpet was installed in Pumpkin Creek United Church on Thursday, and I do not rest in my usual spot anymore. Odd to me, the men could not place me back in the position I held for sixty-eight years. Now, I am the seventeenth pew from the front on the left side of the sanctuary.

Linda Gaines shifts her eyes and smirks when the Williams family wanders into the church for the Sunday evening service. "My goodness." Linda strokes her blonde, coiffed hair. "I hope their daughter doesn't vomit on our gold carpet."

Two church members, Janie and Beverly, stand beside Linda and me. They watch the family find a pew five rows in front of us. With about one-third the congregation showing up for the evening service, the people, especially the teenagers, spread out amongst the pews.

Linda frowns. "Sandy loves corned beef hash, and Marie lets her eat the food all the time." After fostering, Andrew and Marie Williams adopted three children—Billy, Sandy, and Mike.

Beverly, older than Linda and Janie, says, "No, she doesn't."

"Oh?" Linda arches her brows. "My children and I were over at Marie's house two days last week. Guess what she fed us for lunch?"

"Corned beef hash." Janie wrinkles her nose.

Linda nods. "Since the adoption, Sandy's thrown up twice in here." She wrinkles her nose. "And the sour smell lingers in the sanctuary."

Two years ago, when the Gaines family had graced us with their presence, a lady said they resembled models who had stepped off the Sears catalog pages. With pearls at her neck and a pale blue dress with a matching purse and heels, the women flocked to Linda. Quite a few women learned outward appearances were deceiving. Linda's personality did not match her fashion style. A traveling salesman, Mr. Gaines is out of town most Sundays. However, I appreciate when he attends because he is much nicer than Linda.

Humans and carpet are not the only changes at Pumpkin Creek United Church. With the money Benjamin and Suzanne Ward left the church after their deaths, the pastor's study was redecorated and an addition built. Behind the pulpit area and the wall where the cross hangs, a back hallway, six Sunday school classes, and a men's restroom at one end and a ladies' restroom at the other, were constructed. Over the years, Pumpkin Creek United Church has grown and changed from the one-room church I remember.

Beverly puckers her lips and says, "I thought you were friends with Marie."

"I am." Linda adjusts the pearls at her neck. "Jenny plays with Sandy, and Joey plays with Billy, but I'll have to put a stop to that."

"Why?" Beverly lifts a brow.

"Billy gets into trouble at school. Marie and Andrew met

with the principal. Again"—she pauses and leans forward—"when you adopt children, you never know what you're getting."

Billy was dropped off on the front step of a children's home. Sandy and Mike's parents were reported to social services by a neighbor in their apartment building. The two were left at home all day alone and several nights a week. When social services arrived, Mike and Sandy had passed out from dehydration and lack of food.

Janie nods. "That's true."

With a curt voice, Beverly says, "I don't agree. My cousin and her husband adopted a baby girl six years ago, and she's delightful." Beverly places her purse and Bible down on the pew behind me before she straightens. "Maybe with three children, corned beef hash is all they can afford right now. Remember, Marie gave up her position as a third-grade teacher to stay home and raise her children." A pink tinge stains Linda's cheeks, and Beverly continues, "Those of us who have attended the church for years, understand what Marie and Andrew have gone through to have children."

Linda's blush deepens.

"That's true too." A very agreeable Janie nods again. I hope one day, she stands up with confidence to her so-called friend, Linda.

"I know what I hear and see." Linda crosses her arms, drops them, and smiles over Beverly's shoulder. "Hi, Preacher Poythress."

Preacher Poythress has served as interim pastor since Pastor Dunn accepted a teaching position at Moody Bible Institute. A widowed, gentleman in his late fifties, the preacher is known for biblical teaching and a friendship with evangelist Billy Graham.

"Hello, ladies." Preacher Poythress waves a hand, strides toward the Williams family, stops, and chats with the them.

I wonder if the pastor overheard Linda's snide comments about the Williams' children.

Linda cuts her eyes toward the pastor and back at her friends. "Have you noticed he makes an effort to talk to those kids?" Linda's arms cross her chest again.

"He does?" Janie bites the corner of her mouth and releases her lip. "I suppose he talks to mine too. I haven't paid much attention."

Beverly lifts an eyebrow. "Maybe he likes those children."

Linda puts a hand on a hip. "He had Sunday dinner with Andrew and Marie last week. I've asked him twice to join us for Sunday dinner, and he always says another time." She snorts. "I hope Marie didn't serve hash."

Beverly frowns at Linda and sits on the pew behind me.

In her early thirties, not married, and petite, Ethel Louise Thatcher, a direct descendant of Pastor John Everett Thatcher and the youngest sister of Floyd Owen Thatcher, the baby who was delivered on me the day I was shot, walks into the sanctuary. She says a brief hello to the ladies and continues to a pew three rows up from us and across the aisle.

During a business meeting when the members discussed carpet, Linda informed us her previous church had covered their hardwood floors with rugs. She said carpet made all the difference in the world in regards to sound. Even though Ethel Louise voted for carpet, she questioned the required maintenance which did not win her any points with Linda. Other women remained silent on the subject staying on Linda's good side, and I heard, to ensure they keep getting invited to her home for lunch or to play Bridge.

I must say, in the service this morning, the carpet did soften the footsteps of those who made their way to the altar during our closing hymn, "Just As I Am." Still, Linda hurts folks with her unkind remarks, and since God is omniscient, He will teach Linda a lesson in His time.

Preacher Poythress steps behind the pulpit, and Janie glances toward the front. "He's about to begin the service." She steps around her children and sits on me. A stiff-backed Linda edges down near my armrest.

Like every pastor, the preacher follows the normal order of events and opens the evening service. After a short prayer and hymn, the pastor motions for the congregation to take a seat.

"I'm going to do something different tonight." He pauses and the small crowd appears even more attentive. "I've heard conversations over the last few weeks from our members, and God has convicted me. I'm going to share a story with you." His gaze sweeps across the pews and stops on the adoptive children. Four-year-old Sandy waves at the preacher, and he waves back. "Tonight will be informal. If you have questions, feel free to ask them."

This is a first. I wonder what the pastor has to say.

The pastor does not open his Bible. "I'm going to share where I came from, and the purpose God has for me." He looks down and back up. "Too many of us have high opinions of our self which is not of God. And, I don't want any of you to have a high opinion of me. I'm a simple, servant of God. I've traveled with renowned evangelists in my lifetime, and I thank God for those opportunities. Now, He has led me here for a time. I want you all to remember one thing about me." He holds up one finger and pauses, making sure everyone is paying attention. "Remember, I will always speak the truth."

"I appreciate honesty." Beverly says under her breath. Linda glances over her shoulder.

"I was born into poverty." Preacher Poythress grips the pulpit. "My mom died when I was five years old, leaving me and my two older brothers in our dad's care." He pauses a moment. "My father wasn't a nice man. He drank too much. He left us for days at a time with no food or money. Sometimes my older brother would sneak into someone's garden and steal food for us."

Ronnie Sanders remarks, "God had a great plan for you, pastor." Ronnie works with his father on their pig farm which now supplies pork to grocery stores in eastern North Carolina. As for his brother, Wiley Sanders joined the military when he was eighteen and is in everyone's prayers because the Vietnam War does not appear to be ending soon.

"He did." The pastor places a hand on the Bible. "When dad left, my older brothers dropped me at the boarding house in town. The lady who ran the house always fed me and made me work for my keep." The pastor's face drops. "When my dad found out where I was, he'd be mad as a hornet and would yank me by the arm all the way back home saying his son didn't need charity. He didn't know, but I appreciated all the charity I received back then."

With a thick voice, Ethel Louise says, "That's sad."

The local high school history teacher, Ethel Louise is one of my favorite people, and I am her preferred pew until Linda took over sitting on me. Ethel Louise would never start an argument over me, her beloved pew. Even though, I have seen members ask others to move from 'their' pew. A solid Christian woman and role model to the young girls, Ethel Louise is not swayed by the likes of Linda Gaines.

From under the pew in front of the Williams family, three-year-old Mike mutters, "Peacha, peacha." He scoots under the pews toward the front. Marie and Andrew jump up searching for him.

Billy kneels and looks under the pews. "Up there, Mama." The congregation laughs. Billy stands and watches.

"See?" Linda comments over her shoulder at Beverly.

"Never know what you're going to get." Linda's daughter doodles on the morning bulletin, and Joey fiddles with an ink pen. "Be still, Joey." Linda refocuses forward not seeing her son stick his tongue out at her.

The preacher steps from the podium, reaches down, and scoops Mike into suit-clad arms. "Marie and Andrew, have a seat. Mike can stay up here with me." The couple return to their seat with Sandy and Billy perched between them.

"Hi there, young fellow." Preacher Poythress squeezes Mike who wraps small arms around the pastor's neck for a quick hug. "Folks, I cannot remember a time when my father hugged me. Sometimes, I wondered why I was born." The preacher stands in front of the altar steps holding Mike. "Eventually, my oldest brother was arrested and taken away. I've never found him. After a beating from my father one night, my middle brother ran away. Two days later, my father left."

With her index finger, Janie wipes at the corner of an eye. Sniffles sound from women in the crowd.

"I lived in a sad situation." The pastor shifts Mike to the other arm. "You never know what someone is going through. With no one around and no food, I cried my heart out and wandered down to the boarding house." The preacher hesitates. "The lady called the police, and I ended up in an orphanage."

Mike cannot hold sleepy eyes open, and the preacher lays him on the front pew. Marie rises, but the pastor waves her away.

Preacher Poythress steps near the altar table. "Do you all believe children are precious in God's sight?"

"Yes," a man says, and his wife raises her hand in affirmation.

"Of course," Linda acknowledges and pats her daughter on the head. Her husband is away on business again.

"Good. Psalms 127:4 tells us, 'Behold, children are a gift of the Lord, The fruit of the womb is a reward.' So, no matter who births the children, they are a gift and should be treated as such."

Her voice firm, Ethel Louise says, "Amen."

"In the orphanage, I had a roof over my head and food every day." The preacher pauses. "I wasn't always treated with kindness."

"How 'bout school?" Leonard tosses out. "Wish I'd done better in school, but I quit."

A surprise to some, Leonard is alive and kicking despite the life he lived prior to accepting Jesus as Savior.

"We had school too." Preacher Poythress smiles. "I liked school, especially English."

The pastor explains life at the orphanage was not all fun and games. Chores were divvied between the children. Older kids picked on those younger. The staff required obedience. If rules were not followed, the rod was not spared. And, when a couple visited with adoption in mind, the children lined up across the front porch waiting and hoping for a ma and pa.

"We all wished they would pick us." Preacher Poythress looks at Billy and Sandy. "Rejection stared us in the face every day at the home."

Billy snuggles closer to Marie. "I'm glad you picked me." She wraps an arm around him.

"Me too," Sandy says. Across the top of their children's heads, Andrew and Marie share a smile.

"At the orphanage," the pastor steps behind the pulpit, "most of us came from unhappy situations. I believe the staff did the best they could." He fiddles with the Bible's edge. "One boy arrived undernourished. The older kids shared their food with him. One girl wet the bed every night. Over half of the kids were afraid of the dark. Two older girls soothed them until they fell asleep." He chokes up and grasps the pulpit with both hands. "Having food three times a day was a blessing. I'd gobble down whatever was placed on my plate, get sick, and run outside to throw up."

Sandy gasps and slaps a hand over her mouth.

Janie glances at Linda the same time Beverly clears her throat. Linda stares straight ahead. I hope the preacher's words convict and cause her to think before speaking about adopted children. And others.

Preacher Poythress glances Sandy's way. "I soon realized scarfing down my food wasn't necessary anymore. They fed us."

Billy grins. "I love my mama's spaghetti."

Sandy straightens, a grin on her face. "I love corned beef hash with crackers."

"Kiddos, I haven't seen any food I don't like."

Murmurs of agreement resonate around the sanctuary.

The pastor's eyes brighten. "One Sunday afternoon, the Poythress family visited the orphanage. Mr. Poythress was a doctor blessed with three little girls. They couldn't have any more children, and these girls wanted a big brother."

Billy's eyes widen. "They picked you, didn't they, cause your last name is Poythress."

The pastor laughs. "Yes, they picked me." He recalls the day. "I was twelve and had given up on being adopted. The two youngest girls took to me and followed me around all afternoon. The orphaned kids played a ragtag game of softball, which gave me a chance to show the Poythress girls how to throw a ball." The pastor chuckles. "By the time they left, the girls' dresses were covered in dust, and their pigtails were falling out." Preacher Poythress pauses. "I couldn't tell you why they chose me. I was worse for wear."

"Why?" Billy says.

"I had a shaved head because lice had gone through the orphanage a week prior. Two of my back teeth were rotting. I had a broken index finger because I fought with an older boy." The preacher pulls at his collar. "Those were the physical scars. I'd never been shown love, and I sometimes mistrusted others. Not to mention, I was disobedient."

Sandy crawls onto her dad's lap. "My stomach hurts."

"Uh-oh." Linda murmurs. I guess the pastor's words did not resonate with her.

Preacher Poythress surveys the folks. "We are here to serve God and each other. We all have a past and come from different backgrounds. If you're a believer in Jesus, we are brothers and sisters in Christ. We don't have time for pettiness, gossip, or being unkind to each other." He smacks the stand. The crowd straightens. "I will not tolerate this kind of behavior in our church. If you cannot say something nice, be quiet."

Beverly raises a hand heavenward. "Praise the Lord."

The preacher recites Galatians chapter five, verses twenty-two through twenty-three. "'But the fruit of the Spirit is love, joy, peace, patience, kindness, goodness, faithfulness, gentleness, self-control; against such things there is no law.'" He looks over the congregation. "Doctor and Mrs. Poythress lived the fruit of the Spirit and showered me with those fruits. Sometimes in our own church, I can't tell the Christians from the unbelievers, the way we speak of our fellow brothers and sisters in Christ."

No one says a word and looks are passed around. Janie slices a sidelong glance toward Linda.

The silence is thick, a knife could cut through the stillness.

Preacher Poythress nods at the pianist, the crowd stands and sings the closing hymn, and the pastor says the benediction.

When the prayer ends, Sandy nudges past Billy and Marie.

She rushes into the aisle. Sandy slaps her hands over her mouth and runs. She stops dead in her tracks beside me. Sandy hurls. Undigested corn beef hash and mushy crackers hit the new gold carpet.

Linda shrieks. "The carpet."

From behind, Marie grabs Sandy's hair and holds strands away from her face.

"Aww." A youngster steps around the mess.

Preacher Poythress holds a sleepy Mike. He walks up the aisle stopping between Andrew and Billy. He remains a few steps away from the vomit.

"Are you okay?" Marie says.

Tears shine in Sandy's eyes. "Sorry."

The preacher waves a hand. "Oh humbug, we've all thrown up."

Marie releases Sandy's hair. "Maybe we should take a break from corned beef hash."

"No, Mommy," Sandy pleads. "I just ate too much at supper."

"Okay." Marie gives Sandy a quick hug. "I'll make sure we always have corned beef hash in our home. Sound good?"

Sandy nods, looks at the bile on the carpet, and up at those around her.

Beverly pushes a strand of hair away from Sandy's face. "Don't you worry. Carpet can be cleaned, sweetie."

"Our new carpet." Linda huffs and holds out an arm blocking her children. "Kids don't step in the vomit. Joey, get wet rags."

"No way. I ain't cleaning up puke." Joey jumps over my seatback and escapes out the door.

Linda barks at her friend. "Janie, we need this cleaned up before the vomit stains."

"You know where the cleaning supplies are." Janie stands with a hand on her hip.

Linda whips her head toward Janie. "Excuse me?"

Janie holds her ground. "You heard me."

Good for you, Janie, I long to shout.

"As I recall," Janie glares at Linda, "last week when our two families were to clean the church, you were too busy to help. You clean the vomit." Janie takes her youngest daughter by the hand and leaves with her other two children following close behind.

With a slight smile on her face, Ethel Louise hands wet rags over to Linda. "Here you go."

Beverly's smile matches Ethel Louise's. "Appears Linda has everything under control." She looks at Marie and Andrew. "Y'all get the children to the car. Marie, I'll grab your purse." The Williams family heads out, and the preacher waits for Beverly.

When Beverly returns with Marie's purse, the pastor says in Linda's direction, "Since you had a lot of input on choosing the carpet, I'm sure you know more than the rest of us on the best method of cleaning the rug. Thanks for your help."

Linda stares at him. "I ... I ... uh, yes ... I guess."

Leonard looks down and up. "I cleaned these floors years ago when we didn't have carpet. Glad I don't have da clean dat." He shakes his head and walks out.

Beverly gathers her belongings from the pew behind me. "A good, simple lesson tonight, Pastor. Folks needed to hear those words."

Beverly and Preacher Poythress exit the church, leaving Linda and me. She looks down at the vomit. A deathlike shade of white overtakes her skin. Linda slaps a hand over her mouth and swallows.

Good. I did not want her to vomit too. Although I am not the judge of humans, I do appreciate this turn of events.

Until the carpet was replaced, a stain remained on the section of the rug where Sandy heaved. Every time Preacher Poythress walked down the aisle, he glanced at the spot and smiled. I do believe Preacher Poythress knew the likes of humans akin to Linda, and we never heard Linda mention asking the pastor to Sunday dinner again.

13

1973: THE MISCHIEVOUS PAPA PAT

"Marie, please have a talk with your son," a disgruntled Mrs. Watkins says. "If he brings another frog, bug, or slimy thing into my Sunday school class, I'm going to scream."

Billy slips past the two women, steps into the row in front of me, and sits with Sandy and Mike.

Marie glares at him. "Andrew and I'll take care of the situation." Mrs. Watkins huffs at Marie's words before turning away and finding her usual Sunday morning pew.

Marie points a finger at Billy. "Did you bring the dirty frog you found in the driveway to church?" She thrusts her hands on her hips. "Tell me the truth."

Eyes wide, Sandy and Mike gaze at their brother. Behind the Williams' children, sit Papa Pat and Vera, their surrogate grandparents. Vera and Papa Pat's grandchildren live in Florida, their visits are few and far between.

I will never forget the look of horror on Linda Gaines's face as she cleaned up Sandy's vomit. The following year, Mr. Gaines was transferred to another city, so the Gaines family time at Pumpkin Creek United Church was short-lived. I hope Linda learned a valuable lesson *that* night—casting snide remarks can be as bad as casting stones.

Since the Gaines family relocation, Ethel Louise enjoys me again as do Vera and Pat. If Pat had his way, he would sit on the back row or not come at all.

Papa Pat chuckles. "Way to go, Billy."

Billy grins at his partner in crime.

"Hush your mouth." Vera swats a hand at Papa Pat. "Can't you see Marie is trying to get him to behave."

"Last week a cockroach." Marie shivers. "What's next, a snake?" She pauses. "Can I trust you to sit here and keep an eye on your brother and sister?" Marie clucks her tongue. "Never mind. Sandy and Mike will take care of themselves. Please don't cause a ruckus while your father and I sing in the choir."

Before he answers, Papa Pat says, "Oh, he'll be fine. I'm here." Billy, Sandy, and Mike face him.

Marie rolls her eyes. "That doesn't make me feel much better."

Vera waves for Marie to head to the choir. "The children will be fine. I'll watch over them."

"Thanks, Mrs. Vera." Marie gives Billy the "you better behave stare." She walks to the pews on the podium reserved for the choir members.

Papa Pat pulls chewing gum from a pocket. "Look what I have." He hands each kid a piece.

When the children open the wrappers and toss the gum into their mouths, Vera looks at them. "Don't let me hear you popping gum, or I'll pull your ears." Papa Pat pops a stick into his mouth.

I wait and wish with all my strength gum had never been invented because in a few minutes when the kids finish chewing the sweetness from the gum, they will stick the residue under their seat pew. Unfortunate for me, my seat bottom has as much goo as the other pews. I find the gunk disgusting.

Papa Pat smacks his gum. Vera reaches for his ear. Papa Pat grabs her hand and places light kisses on her fingertips. As usual, Papa Pat's smacking embarrasses Vera. What is more, he mortifies her with comical remarks about the preacher and others or, worse yet, falls asleep during a sermon. Vera has been known to poke him in the ribs during a service. I hope he does not jump up one Sunday from a nap and cause an uproar.

Gripping my armrest, Papa Pat leans forward. "Billy, did you put the frog in Mrs. Watkin's chair?"

Billy looks around, searching for other listening ears. "He wiggled out of my hand and jumped on Rhonda's lap. She screamed and slapped the frog away." He giggles around the mound of gum. "Then that crazy toad landed on Mrs. Watkins' Bible. I thought she was gonna faint."

"You'll want to stop bringing bugs and such. Girls aren't too fond of those things. Although," Papa Pat places an index finger on his clean-shaven cheek, "I do have earthworms in my garden."

Billy's eyes widen, and he gulps around the gum. "I wanna see those."

"I'm kidding. If you brought those in, I'd never hear the end of Vera's wrath." Papa Pat nods in the direction of Vera. "Oops, time to hush up." He looks toward the podium. "Here comes the old stick in the mud."

Billy glances forward, and Dr. Luther steps behind the pulpit. "Ugh. He's boring."

Papa Pat chuckles. "Maybe you need to visit the Pentecostal church. They do what's called the three S's: Stomping, spitting, and shouting. Although Luther grows hot under the collar if things don't go his way."

"You're tellin' me." Billy shifts facing Papa Pat. "At the last youth cookout, I grabbed a match and threw the thing on the grill because Dad lets me light our grill when we cook out. I knew what I was doing, but Luther was furious. I thought his head would explode. He grabbed my arm and was about to whack me."

Complaints about Dr. Luther abound within the church. I notice Billy, along with a few other members, neglect the courtesy title, doctor, in front of Dr. Luther's name. I suspect they do not respect our pastor.

Papa Pat straightens. "Was your dad around?"

"Oh yeah. Dad grabbed Luther's arm and told him he'd better not lay a hand on me. Said if he ever touched one of us, Dad would have a come to Jesus meeting with him behind the church." Billy rolls unforgiving eyes. "I still had to apologize for throwing a match on the grill. Afterward, Dad explained how men tend their own barbeques, and next time, I should ask before I intrude on another man's grill."

"Andrew's a good father," Papa Pat says.

Billy scratches the side of his nose. "Luther hasn't talked to Dad since the cookout."

Voted in by the congregation, Dr. Luther replaced Preacher Poythress. Dr. Luther is strict. He likes things his way. If anyone makes a noise, clears their throat too much, or heads for the restroom during a sermon, he asks you to leave. The singled-out individual is embarrassed right in front of the entire congregation.

Do not get me started on Dr. Luther's sermons about miniskirts, boys with long hair, and television. On Sunday nights, he demands all teenagers sit in the first three rows because he wants to keep an eye on them. And, he proclaims television is the "devil's tool" and not allowed in the Luthers' home.

I still do not understand how he was voted in as our pastor.

Most sermons are a hellfire and brimstone nature, and a majority of members have remarked the pastor needs more variety when he preaches. I too wish he would choose another topic.

When Dr. Luther stands behind the pulpit, parents keep a firm grip on their children hoping to prevent embarrassment. I am glad Andrew and Marie will return to their seats after the choir sings their special music. I do not want Billy, Sandy, or Mike getting into any trouble with the preacher. In all my years here, Dr. Luther has been, by far, the most arrogant, opinionated, and harshest of preachers. I expect our pastor will not last too much longer at our church.

Dr. Luther looks out, the congregation sits at attention, and all is quiet. He looks down at a sheet of paper in his hands. "The announcements—"

Ribbit.

Oh my, Billy and the frog.

Billy's eyes widen. He slaps a hand against the pew. Sandy stares at him. Mike bursts into giggles.

Ribbit.

Mrs. Watkins turns her head and glares at Billy. Marie's face turns bright red. Papa Pat puts a fist in front of smiling lips.

Mike jumps up and points. "The frog's on the floor. Get him."

"I'm trying." Billy leaps up, reaches down, and grabs the frog. He stands in the pew row holding the small creature and glancing around.

Dr. Luther scowls at Billy. "What's going on?"

Billy darts a look toward Papa Pat, his parents, and back at Dr. Luther. "I ... I ... you see ..."

From the choir, Andrew says, "You still have the frog from this morning?"

With downcast eyes, Billy nods.

Papa Pat motions over his shoulder at the door. "Everything's okay. Billy, take the frog outside and let him go."

"Excuse me, Pat. I'll handle this." Dr. Luther puts one hand on the pulpit. Papa Pat sits erect. The preacher turns toward the choir and focuses on Andrew. "You need to get your house under control."

Folks gasp. With nostrils flaring, Andrew draws in dark eyebrows. Marie pops up, maneuvers around choir members, and heads toward her children.

"My house is fine." Andrew rises and follows Marie.

Papa Pat jumps onto his feet. "Amen."

"Oh brother," Vera murmurs under her breath. I guess she knows, and I suspect, Papa Pat is about to make a spectacle of himself.

"In the Lord's house, I demand you show respect." The preacher slams a fist down. Several folks jolt up straighter in their seats. Others look around in dismay.

Dr. Luther's wife speaks up from the front pew. "Please, Tom—"

He glares at her. "I'm the leader in this church."

Billy peers at Papa Pat. Tears sting Sandy's eyes. Anger stains Andrew and Marie's faces. They approach their children.

Vera tilts her head, gazes at Pat, and asks loud enough for those close by to hear, "What're you doing?"

No spring chicken, Papa Pat acts fast. "Oh ... oh ..." He clutches his chest with a hand and the pew in front of me with the other. "My ... my heart." Papa Pat glances at Vera, staggers into the aisle, and drops on the floor. He must be in excruciating pain.

Vera jumps out of her seat, mouth agape. Other members leap up. With a puzzled expression on her face, Vera kneels beside Papa Pat. Choir members stand and watch the situation unfolding before their eyes. Dr. Luther stands on the podium, jowls shaking, and mouth hanging open.

Vera squints, takes Papa Pat's hand, and leans beside his face. "Are you serious ... about your heart?"

"I couldn't let him," Papa Pat cuts eyes toward the preacher, and in a lowered voice, I hear, "rebuke Billy in front of everyone."

"Papa Pat." Mike cries. "Is he gonna be okay, Mama?" Sandy clasps her mother's hand. Marie does not answer.

Vera darts her eyes at those gathering around. Since she is near me, I hear her say, "I cannot believe you're doing this."

Papa Pat groans. "My heart."

With frog in hand, Billy stands near Papa Pat's feet and stares at his surrogate granddad.

"Henry, call an ambulance," Deacon Leroy calls out to the man.

Pushing folks aside, Henry rushes toward the pastor's study located off the vestibule.

Dr. Luther hurries down from the podium as fast as his plump body will move. He stops behind Vera. "Pat, I ... I ..."

Vera grimaces, and I guess she decides to join in Papa Pat's charade. "Can you ..." Vera clears her throat. "Can you breathe?"

Papa Pat nods and closes his eyes.

Deacon Leroy kneels and places a hand over Papa Pat's chest. "Heart's beating."

"Whew." Billy exhales. Sighs escape from others around the sanctuary.

Deacon Leroy points toward the front door. "Make sure the medical team can get through the parking lot and in here." Following the deacon's instruction, two men rush outside.

Dr. Luther pushes a lady aside and kneels on one knee beside Vera. "Let me pray over him." Vera directs a hard glare at the preacher who looks away from her. "Folks, let's pray."

Members sit nearby, bow down at their pew, or stand in the church aisle. Behind Vera, Marie and Andrew stop with Sandy and Mike between them. Billy hovers where he is, never taking eyes off Papa Pat. Whispered prayers resonate. Dr. Luther raises an arm and shouts a prayer heavenward, the preacher's voice drowning out the other softspoken prayers.

Papa Pat opens his eyes, glances around, and finds Billy. He forms a fist near his waistband, looks back and forth from Billy to his fist, and gives a quick thumbs up. He lifts his brows and smiles. Billy nods and returns the smile.

I believe the 'heart attack' is an extreme, mischievous act to avoid Dr. Luther's wrath. However, the preacher is rather mean.

"... in Jesus's name. Amen." Dr. Luther finishes, and amens echo around the sanctuary at the exact moment two members hold the door open for two volunteer emergency workers.

Andrew waves both arms. "Everyone move back. Give them room."

Folks make a path for the workers. Marie, Sandy, and Mike take three steps backward. Mothers with small children move away from all the activity. Teens gather between the pews and talk amongst themselves. With a crying baby in the mother's arms, one young couple gathers their belongings and exits the church. Billy does not budge.

The volunteers, dressed in jeans and casual shirts, push a gurney with medical gear stuffed on top and stop beside Papa Pat.

Deacon Leroy stands and addresses a worker. "Dennis, we think Pat's had a heart attack." The emergency workers are volunteers from the community. I recognize Dennis but not the younger man whose long, blonde hair is pulled back into a ponytail. The workers kneel beside Papa Pat and open medical cases.

Dennis directs the younger worker, "Chad, check his blood pressure." Chad removes a blood pressure cuff from a case and places the band around Papa Pat's arm. Vera moves down toward her husband's right shin out of the way of the medical technicians. Dennis uses a stethoscope and listens to Papa Pat's heart.

Chad's mouth pulls in a corner. "Hmmm. Blood pressure appears normal for a man his age."

Dennis says, "Heart sounds good too." He settles an oxygen mask over Papa Pat's nose and mouth.

Papa Pat remains alert, eyes shifting and looking at those around him. Billy focuses on him, the frog still in hand. Papa Pat pulls the mask away. "I feel better."

"Do you now?" Vera points at Papa Pat. "Put the mask back on." Her face flushes. Oh boy, Papa Pat will be in heaps of trouble with Vera.

Chad jerks up. "I forgot the small case." He dashes out the door.

Billy kneels at Papa Pat's side. "You *are* okay, right?" Papa Pat indicates for Billy to lean closer. He removes the mask and whispers. The two chuckle, and he replaces the mask. When Billy stands, the frog leaps from his hand. Billy twists and searches on hands and knees. "Where did he go?"

"Good grief." Dr. Luther's nostrils flare.

Billy looks around people's feet. "I can't find him."

An older woman jumps back. A young girl crouches on the pew across the aisle.

A man points. "Over here."

Billy jumps up, collides into the gurney, regains balance, and reaches for the frog.

Ribbit.

Dr. Luther glowers. "You and that frog. Get him out of here."

"Grab him," Marie says.

Too late. The frog high tails down the remainder of the center aisle. A man in his seventies reaches for the frog. He misses. The frog vanishes from sight. Billy maneuvers around folks, chasing after the ribbit.

Billy looks over a shoulder. "He went under the door to the preacher's study."

"The door's locked," Dr. Luther yells out. "You're not allowed in there."

Papa Pat leans up.

Dennis pushes Papa Pat's shoulder. "Please lay back down."

Vera tosses Papa Pat a hard look. "Listen to the man." Glancing at Dennis, she says, "Maybe my husband needs a shot." With speed, Papa Pat shakes his head in response.

Chad returns with the small case and settles beside their patient. He unbuttons the top buttons of Papa Pat's shirt, removes several cords from the case, and attaches them on Papa Pat's chest.

Dennis checks Papa Pat's pulse and listens to his heart again. "Heart still sounds fine."

Billy calls out. "I don't believe what I see."

"What now?" Andrew asks.

Within moments, Billy walks farther into the sanctuary and stops a couple of feet away from Papa Pat.

A small boy points. "Look."

Billy grins from ear to ear. He holds a small television set with an antenna protruding from the top part.

Andrew's eyes narrow at the preacher. "My, my, my, what have we here?"

Papa Pat swats at the medical technician's hands, sits up,

and scoots backward against the pew across from me watching this turn of events. Dennis scowls, and Chad shrugs.

Dr. Luther's cheeks turn crimson. "You have no business in my office."

Billy gawks at the preacher. "You have no business with a TV."

Henry's eyes bulge. "I unlocked the office door and called the ambulance. I must've forgotten to lock the door back." Deacons have keys for all the doors, interior and exterior. Too bad for Dr. Luther. "I didn't notice the television. I was in such a hurry to get back in here."

"Folks, folks." Sweat covers Dr. Luther's balding head.

Papa Pat rips off the oxygen mask and drops the plastic covering on the floor. Dennis retrieves the mask and attempts to replace the covering over Papa Pat's nose and mouth. Papa Pat pushes Dennis's arm away, snickers, and points. "A television. I thought TVs were the 'devil's tool'?" Several folks comment in agreement, cross their arms, and glare at the preacher.

Mrs. Luther's eyes turn hard. "That's what my husband preaches."

With thick jowls trembling, Dr. Luther points at Billy. "You."

Andrew roars at the preacher. "Now wait a minute."

Billy smirks. "The television shouldn't be in your office."

Dr. Luther loosens his tie, reaches for a handkerchief, and wipes his head. The church is now full of misguided folks and a flustered Dr. Luther.

The preacher's wife shakes her head. "Tom, I cannot believe you."

Dr. Luther's cheeks bulge. They remind me of the red balloons with too much air about to pop that I once saw the youngsters use in a skit. "What do you know?"

Mrs. Luther puts her hands on her hips. "I don't preach one thing and do another."

"I needed the television for research."

Papa Pat snorts. "Huh, that's a pile of baloney."

Dr. Luther's wife scowls. "I suppose you spend time over here and watch television?"

Dennis closes a case. "We need to get him to the hospital."

"Hold on." A wicked smile crosses Papa Pat's face. "Like I thought, a man talking out of two sides of his mouth."

"Pat." With wide eyes, Vera nods with persistence. "You should go to the hospital."

Papa Pat holds up a finger. "One more minute."

Billy shifts the small television under an arm. "What do you want me to do with this?"

Before anyone utters a word, Mrs. Luther says, "You can have the TV."

Billy looks at his dad. "Can I?"

"Yep," Andrew says, and Billy grins.

"Folks, please step aside." Dennis pushes a hand backwards indicating the crowd should listen to him. "We're gonna get him on the gurney and to the hospital." He looks at Papa Pat. "You need to listen to us." Dennis and Chad lift Papa Pat placing him on the gurney.

While Chad gathers the medical cases, Papa Pat motions for Billy. "Come here."

"We need to go," Dennis says.

Papa Pat holds up a finger. "I will. A second, please."

Billy stops beside the gurney and props the television against the stretcher.

"Where's the frog?" Papa Pat asks Billy.

"I left him in Dr. Luther's office."

"Good. Remember the earthworms?" Papa Pat's eyes light

up. "The frog will need company." He winks at Billy, and Vera close by, rolls her eyes.

Uh-oh, more mischief. Maybe, Dr. Luther deserves the naughtiness.

Vera's voice rises. "Get him out of here."

"Clear the aisle. Make way." Deacon Leroy leads the way with Dennis and Chad maneuvering the gurney behind him. Vera follows. Billy stares after them.

When they exit, Marie steps next to Billy and places an arm around her son's shoulders. "He'll be fine."

Billy looks into her face and bursts into giggles. "Oh yes, he will."

Marie takes a deep breath and sighs. "Oh no, what has Papa Pat done now?"

The next Sunday a special business meeting is called, and Dr. Luther is voted out. Papa Pat attends, and I am not surprised. I imagine wild horses could not have kept him away.

After all was said and done, and as a select few knew, Papa Pat did not have a heart attack, but he acted the role with gusto. Maybe he should have won an Academy Award. If Papa Pat had known what his antics would unveil, I expect he would have performed the act sooner. The doctors diagnosed the 'chest pain' as gas. Papa Pat faked the heart attack and protected his surrogate grandson from the wrath of Dr. Luther. I believe God used Papa Pat to reveal Dr. Luther's secret in His way.

Because God knows all.

14

1986: TROY'S GONE FISHIN'

*A*fter replacing Dr. Luther and serving thirteen years at Pumpkin Creek United Church, Pastor Boseman's attire has shifted from the seventies to the eighties. The pastor stands on the podium in a white, double-breasted suit. Yes, white. A pale, green shirt with a pink and green tie add character to the ensemble.

As folks arrived, a lady said the preacher dressed identical to Sonny Crockett from the television series, "Miami Vice." I do not care how the pastor dresses because he cares for our flock, and if any member or family is in need, Pastor Boseman shares the burden.

Dark circles show beneath the pastor's eyes. "Folks, we have a miracle in our midst. Last night was a long night for the Parker family." Pastor Boseman focuses on Troy Parker.

During the morning's opening hymn, Troy, Ruth, and their three teenaged children entered the church and sat on the front pew, left side. Odd, because I have never seen Troy near the front of the church. Middle-aged with sagging shoulders and an arm bandaged to the elbow, deep lines crease Troy's face. Ruth's eyes are puffy and red as are those of her children.

Pastor Boseman looks over the congregation. "Ruth called me last night. She said Troy was missing." With two fingers pointing at Troy, the preacher gestures. "Now, there he sits with Ruth and their teenagers."

The Pumpkin Creek community is an hour and a half's drive from the North Carolina coastline. A number of folks in the church enjoy fishing and spending time at the beach. Yesterday morning, Troy had gone fishing in the Atlantic Ocean and had not returned before sunset. According to the information I have overheard, Troy had promised Ruth he would be home before dark. Troy's two sons contacted the sheriff's office at the beach and the Coast Guard. Pastor Boseman and two deacons rushed over to the Parker home, acquired more details, and prayed with the family. The men remained at their home in support of the family. The sheriff searched the marina and found Troy's empty truck and boat trailer, but no Troy.

Low whispers sound from the congregation.

"Listen," Pastor Boseman motions with his hands, the crowd settles down, and Troy walks forward. "I'm not preaching today. Troy and I have talked. He asked to share the events of yesterday with y'all."

Troy wears rumpled blue slacks and a wrinkled, short-sleeved white dress shirt, not his usual suit and tie, and with measured steps, climbs the three stairs toward Pastor Boseman who hugs him. The preacher relaxes in a winged-back chair set off to the side and behind Troy.

Despite the weariness on Troy's face, he grasps the pulpit, eyes burning bright with conviction. "Today, I want to proclaim, I am a Christian. I believe in Jesus Christ as my Lord and Savior." He taps the pastor's Bible resting on the stand. "I haven't always given a hundred percent here at the church or in my walk with the Lord. That's going to change."

A successful custom-builder in the area, Troy does not go out of the way to serve in the church or lend a helping hand. Ruth, on the other hand, assists with youth outings, helps in the nursery, and provides meals for sick members and others out in the community. She loves the Lord, and Jesus shines through in her words and actions.

"I met Jesus last night and I ..." Troy's voice quivers. "I need to share what happened. I surr ..." He pauses regaining his composure. "I surrendered my life to Christ fully. No more part-time Christianity for me."

Pastor Boseman raises a fist upward.

Humility is not Troy's strong suit. Words such as those have never been uttered from this well-respected and prominent man in our community. Troy's confession makes me wonder the number of other folks who are doing Christianity part-time, not giving God their all or, worse, faking their Christianity.

"Last night, darkness surrounded me." Troy points straight at the stained-glass window showing Jesus on the cross. "I'm thankful for the sunshine pouring through the window."

The clear, glass windows were replaced with beautiful stained-glass ones a few years ago. I had always loved the white walls—clean and fresh—now the colors from the glass streaming across the walls when the sun rises and sets brings a whole new view to my world. Ten years ago, the members replaced the gold carpet with a deep red one and last year added bigger, chandeliers. The church has come a long way from the one-room, wooden structure with candlelight fixtures. And I am proud I still live here despite the changes. Now I sit at the third row on the left.

Troy says, "I thought yesterday would be a nice day for fishing. The sun was out and the ocean calm." He bows his head. The pastor stands and puts an arm around Troy's trembling shoulders.

Ruth snivels and hugs her daughter who sits on her right.

Pastor Boseman whispers near Troy's ear. When he nods, the preacher returns to the chair.

Troy looks over the congregation. "I went fishing when I should have helped you all with Mrs. Anderson's porch." He finds the older lady. "Ruth and my kids helped." Troy faces his family. "I'm proud of you, kids. You did the right thing. I'm sorry I wasn't there. I should've helped."

Yesterday had been set aside for rebuilding Mrs. Anderson's front porch. Not one to ask for charity, Ethel Louise Thatcher, now fifty-one-years old, had approached the pastor and deacons about Mrs. Anderson's need. The men insisted the church would replace and cover the cost.

The pastor says, "We didn't finish the job and could still use your expertise."

"You got it." Troy tosses a smile at the preacher.

Troy shares yesterday started out fine. When he steered the boat for shore everything—the motor, lights, and radio—stopped working. Good with manual work, Troy tinkered with the motor and electronics, but nothing helped. The situation must have been frightening for him although, I am sure God had a plan.

Troy looks down, shakes his head, and refocuses on the audience. "An uneasiness settled over me when the sun set. I realized I'd seen one boat all afternoon."

Ethel Louise, sitting against my right corner, grips my armrest. I enjoy her company because she makes me feel a closeness to those from the Thatcher family who have passed to their eternal home. Her great-grandfather, Joseph Everett Thatcher, crosses my mind.

"Folks, I didn't consider praying." Troy blushes. "That's how arrogant I was."

When the boat sloshed around, Troy grasped at the fiberglass hardtop over the console of his twenty-one-foot, Carolina Skiff boat. Instead, he fell onto the small deck and crawled toward the captain's chair more worried than ever before.

Since I cannot swim, I wonder if I would sink to the bottom of the ocean or float. I say with assurance, I do not want to find out.

Troy pulls at his collar. "Finally, I finagled my way into the life vest, and before the last ray of light faded, I pulled a flashlight from the waterproof emergency pack stored under a boat seat." Wide-eyed, he scans the crowd. "How I didn't fall out of the boat is beyond me."

Troy flicked the beam of light over the water. Waves crashed against the boat. He did not understand the sudden change in the weather.

He looks down and gazes up. "I realized Ruth and the kids would be worried. That's when I said my first prayer, asking God to get me back home safely. I thought about my family and what their plans had been yesterday—to help Mrs. Anderson. I knew Ruth would make her famous brownies for all the volunteers, and she would leave two on the kitchen counter for me." Troy gazes at Ruth and tears slide down his cheeks. "She's always concerned about me, the kids, and others before herself. I don't deserve you."

Sniffs, snivels, and nose-blowing sound throughout the church. Pastor Boseman steps near Troy, reaches for something under the pulpit, hands him a tissue, and returns to the wingedback chair.

Troy uses the tissue and breathes a deep breath. "I was selfish. After working all week, I thought I deserved some 'me' time. I provide for my family. I thought, why not. I'm going fishing."

Sometimes, God must give folks a wakeup call on their priorities in life. Troy received his call last night.

Troy grabbed ropes and tied them around the metal cleats scattered on the upper edge of the boat's sides. He threw the ropes over the side and into the water in case he went overboard. If he went over the side, maybe Troy could grab a rope.

The story reminds me of Jonah.

He shrugs, and I hear the regret in Troy's voice. "I wondered if God was paying me back for not helping with the porch. Would God allow what happened to Jonah, happen to me? If so, no one would ever find me." Troy swallows. "I was scared but still arrogant. That wouldn't happen in our day and age." Troy's left hand grips the pulpit edge, knuckles turning white.

Troy explains how a wave crashed over the side tossing him overboard. He plunged beneath the waves. Rising, head above the swells, he thrashed in the water. The flashlight pressed against the life vest.

"Once I relied on the life vest, I flashed the beam on a rope." Troy lifts the hurt arm a few seconds at waist height. "I grabbed the line and wrapped the rope around my hand and forearm. With my left hand, I held onto the flashlight for dear life." Troy looks over a shoulder at the pastor. "I begged God to save me." He looks at the crowd, shuffles his weight from side to side, and stops. "And then, I heard, 'Why?'"

The congregation listens in silence and at the other end of my pew, a young boy's mouth hangs open.

Troy's voice rises. He speaks fast. "I kicked in circles. Bobbed up and down. Fought the waves. Aimed the light in all directions." He rakes a hand through his hair. "Maybe my mind was playing tricks on me, a weird sound from the waves, or the

Holy Spirit convicting me. I don't know. I was scared to death. With the rope around my arm, I fought the water and pulled myself toward the boat, not letting go of the one light I had. I knew," he pauses, inhales, and releases a long breath, "I'd better get busy praying for deliverance." His lower lip quivers. "I didn't want to die."

I have heard humans think about dying when they are in a tough situation. I wonder why they do not realize they could die at any moment. Dying is, after all, at God's appointed time—not only when the times are tough.

Troy sniffs and prods forward with the story. "Fear and frustration took over my mind and body. I was angry at God." He picks at the edge of the Bible. "I blamed Him for my situation."

Captivated by Troy's night, the single sound in the sanctuary is the low swish of cool air from the air vents.

Troy searches the faces in the audience. "I'd loved the world, not God or what was important in life. I remembered the day I asked Ruth to marry me, and she said yes. Even though, I didn't have money for a diamond engagement ring." He smiles at Ruth. "She still wears her gold wedding band and has never asked for another ring."

Ruth gives her ring finger a quick peck and places her hand over her heart.

"I've tried finding contentment in the things of the world." Troy shakes his head. "Now I know, this world will never bring me real peace and joy."

True contentment comes when humans follow and commit their lives to Jesus.

"I cried and begged God for help." Troy halts, bites his lip, and continues, "Realization hit me. I suddenly thought of myself as a lost believer, like driving across the country without a roadmap. I was lost in the direction I was living my life. I wasn't glorifying God." He points at his chest. "I lived for my satisfaction."

When Troy was a few feet away from the vessel, a huge swell crashed against the boat, and the skiff capsized. The force from the wave pushed Troy under the water. I cannot imagine the fear in Troy's mind when the boat overturned. Last night, if I had been Ruth, my heart would have been in a thousand pieces.

Troy did not know if determination, adrenalin, or the hand of God lifted him up. With the rope still around one hand, and the flickering flashlight in the other, he gasped for breath. Troy would be a goner if the light disappeared, surrounded in darkness with whatever lurked under the dark water.

"The thought of drowning terrified me." Troy swipes at tears. "I gulped salt water, swam this way and that way, and ... dropped the flashlight."

The same young boy sitting on me leans his arms on the pew back in front of us, eyes fixed on Troy, mouth still ajar.

Poor Troy, a night of never-ending terror.

Troy holds up the bandaged arm, fist clenched. "I yelled into the night, mad at myself, mad at God, mad at everything."

Tears roll down Ruth and her three teenager's faces.

Troy rests the bandaged arm on the pulpit. "All of a sudden, the turmoil in the ocean settled, and a sliver of moonlight hit the overturned boat. I yanked and pulled on the rope, my lifeline. The light," he looks heavenward and back, "was an answered prayer."

Troy prayed for a boat or helicopter—the Coast Guard—but rescuing was not yet to be.

"I hovered against the boat hull." Troy wipes a wet cheek. "I cried, hung onto the rope for dear life. I begged God for another chance. I wanted more time with my family. To live my life for Him."

I am glad God rescued Troy, however, not everyone receives a second opportunity.

With eyes wide, the words rush from the boy on my pew. "Wow. You didn't drown."

"I didn't drown." Troy smiles at the boy. "God provided a miracle because I'm standing here."

With a tissue, Ruth dabs at her eyes. Her oldest son swipes a hand down his face.

"Folks, God had my attention." Stepping sideways, he stands before the congregation. Troy lifts the bandaged arm waist high. "I believe what they say when you're in a terrible situation, your life flashes before your face. I knew I needed to stay awake and talk with God, and my words weren't eloquent by any means." Troy lifts both arms up and outward. "With raw hands and arms, and God's strength, I pulled upward and dropped face down on the upturned boat."

Troy returns behind the pulpit, removes another tissue, and wipes his nose. The story and events of last night drain him of strength. However, I believe God is with him.

Troy sticks the tissue in a pocket and gazes at Ruth. "My body and mind were exhausted. I prayed for God to keep me awake. I realized what I had left at home." Troy looks away and hesitates before saying, "I realized how self-centered and greedy I'd been. I shouted at God, Why can't I be more like Ruth, and you know what happened?"

No one answers.

"Five words popped into my mind. Live each day for God." Troy lifts a brow. "First, I confessed my sins which is the easy part. The living each day for God, difficult for me. I mean ..." He stares at the floor, lifts his eyes, and sighs. "I spit out unkind words too fast, and folks say, I'm tightfisted in my business dealings. And, I haven't been the greatest husband or father either."

Amazing, the way God instructs His children. Certain lessons more frightening than others.

The Holy Spirit convicted Troy last night. He prayed for God's direction, a restored relationship with Ruth and their children, and for God to change him into a Christian man who lived his live for Him.

"You all know the song we sing, 'I Surrender All'?" Troy does not wait for an answer. "I sang the chorus over and over last night while sobbing on top of a boat hull. A peace washed over me I've never experienced before in my life. I stopped crying and singing. I laid my head down, on my upside-down boat." A soft chuckle escapes Troy. "I submitted all control over to God, and with the rolling waves, the boat rocked, and I dozed off and on."

Pastor Boseman stands. "Incredible how God works in our lives."

Troy face beams. "The next thing I know, I opened my eyes and saw the search light of the Coast Guard."

"Praise the Lord," the woman seated behind Troy's family says, and several members echo her acclamations.

With the pastor beside him, Troy finishes the story. "Last night seemed an eternity and in reality, lasted a few hours. A few hours of pure hell—lost and lonely. I don't wish my experience on any person. God saved me physically last night, more importantly, He saved me from being a man who does Christianity parttime. Today, I'm a man who desires to put God first every day." He glances at the pastor. "I had to share my story with our congregation." Troy searches out Mrs. Anderson in the congregation again. "My crew will be at your house first thing in the morning. We'll finish your porch."

Mrs. Anderson smiles, and Pastor Boseman places a hand on Troy's shoulder. "The doctors and nurses bandaged Troy's arm and suggested he spend the remainder of last night in the hospital. Troy informed them, he planned to attend church this morning because God laid a testimony upon him. I'm glad you shared your experience with us."

What a privilege hearing Troy's words. I am glad I reside here too.

"I clung onto the rope with this hand last night." Troy extends the bandaged arm as straight as possible heavenward. "I hope the scars never fade. They resemble Jesus with His nail-scarred hands. I want to share what He did for me, how God changed me, with anyone who will listen."

Troy looks at Ruth. His wife and children hurry up the altar steps and hover around him. Joyful tears escape the Parker family while they hug each other.

Last night, Troy turned away from his 'me' attitude and dedicated his life to Christ out in the middle of the ocean.

Praise the Lord, indeed.

Over time, Troy became one of the most active volunteers ever at Pumpkin Creek United Church. I would place him right up there with Leonard Gilstrap. Both men, once God showed them who was in control, were on fire to serve Him.

When God has a plan for you, He will get your attention one way or another. He did with Jonah. And Troy.

15

1999: THE FUNERAL OF JUICY FRUIT JAY

*I*f a pew could cry, I would.

With the altar table moved into a classroom for the funeral, Barbara and Jasper Miller sit on the front pew from the pulpit, staring at the casket holding their fourteen-year-old son, Jay, one of the sweetest, most humble Christians to enter through the Pumpkin Creek United Church doors. I remain at my third row from the front, left side position. I am filled with sorrow, indeed, for this day.

Our current pastor, Randall Freeman, dubbed "Reverend" by his Dallas Cowboy teammates while he studied to become a preacher, stifles a sob into a fist. After a moment, Reverend says, "You shall love the Lord your God with all your heart and with all your soul and with all your might."

Whimpers sound inside the church, which is packed to capacity—two-hundred and eighty-five people. Mourners stand along the side and back walls, not an inch to spare on my seat or any of the other pews.

Reverend cracks a smile. "Jay was the essence of Deuteronomy 6:5. You know, he loved the Lord. Jay's body may have been weak, but his spirit was huge. The grin he wore every time I saw him was one of the biggest testimonies I've ever witnessed."

After playing in the NFL in the 1980s, Reverend left, followed the call into ministry, and became a pastor. He held a position as an associate pastor for three years with a church in Texas before moving his wife and kids to North Carolina. In 1990, during the week of Reverend's interview process, the impressionable young men and women listened in awe when he shared football stories while under the tutelage of Head Coach Tom Landry. I was more impressed with the way Reverend always circled the stories back to how God worked in a football player's life on and off the field.

"I remember my first Sunday here." Large and muscular, Reverend swipes an index finger at the corner of one eye. "Our friend Jay was about five, I guess. He was parked in a wheelchair in the foyer with a basket of gum on his lap." Reverend glances at the Millers and back at the crowd. "I looked at the basket, at him, and said, 'What's up Juicy Fruit?' That was all she wrote. The name stuck, Juicy Fruit Jay. That's what we've called him ever since."

"He loved having a nickname," Jasper speaks up. "After the service on the car ride home, he talked nonstop. You made his day."

Jay loved Wrigley's Juicy Fruit gum and always shared with the other children in the church. Before Reverend's arrival as our pastor, Jay decided he needed a position on the church's welcoming committee. Pastor Boseman, along with Jay's parents, agreed. Each Sunday morning, he sat stationed in a wheelchair in the foyer with a basket full of gum perched on his lap. He handed over a chewy delight to whoever wanted a piece. Jay, who should have a right to be angry, sad, or upset with his circumstances, always sported a huge grin.

"We're here to celebrate Juicy Fruit Jay's life today." Reverend swallows hard. "People have shared with me about their friendship with Jay." The pastor extends both hands outward. "Look around at everyone here. Look at all the lives he touched in a short time on earth."

People turn their heads, glance over their shoulders, or shift their bodies looking at all in attendance.

Reverend grasps the edge of the pulpit. "Children, young folks—everybody—when God sees something in you, you must use your gifts and talents for Him. We all live on borrowed time."

Barbara breaks down into tears, and Jasper pulls her closer into the crook of an arm. Grief stretches through the air. Tears roll down people's faces. Hiccups, sniffles, and sighs escape from the crowd. Then, as if God touches Jay with His finger, rays of sunlight stream through the stained-glass window near the front and fall on Juicy Fruit Jay's lifeless body, brilliance radiating all around him.

Although I have seen sunlight stream through the window on bright days, I am in awe at the moment.

Reverend points at Jay's casket. "The shining rays are a miniscule portion of the light Jay is standing before now. He is with his Savior. He knew Jesus is the Light of the world. I pray you all believe this too."

Diagnosed with Duchenne muscular dystrophy when he was a toddler, Jay suffered muscle loss in both thighs and pelvis. He struggled to walk. A wheelchair was fitted for his small body, and he remained on the church's prayer list his entire life. Now, no more prayers are needed for him.

Reverend's face turns serious. "If you don't have Jesus when you die, you will be separated from the Light." The pastor's gaze floats over the congregation. "Folks, just because you are healthy does not mean you will see tomorrow. Juicy

Fruit Jay lived his days for the Lord. He chose to let his light shine for Jesus." He looks toward a teenage girl. "Now, Lisa will say a few words." Reverend steps aside.

Lisa, and other teenagers sitting in the congregation, grew up in our church. She hopes to one day work with special needs children and always had a special bond with Jay. Her blonde hair hangs down around her shoulders contrasting with the black dress she wears. She steps behind the pulpit and fumbles with the note cards in her hands. After she blots her eyes with a wadded-up tissue, Lisa looks around. "I'm nervous."

"You'll do fine." Reverend pats Lisa's shoulder. "Say what God's placing on your heart."

"Yes, sir." She places the cards on the stand. "I'd written out my thoughts, now, I think I'll share a story, what I remember most about Juicy Fruit Jay, and the way he loved Jesus and others." She fidgets with a card's edge. "When Jay was in the hospital, he was about nine, our middle-school youth group thought up the hair-brained idea of surprising him. We borrowed my mom's seven-foot-tall, artificial Christmas tree and glued hundreds of sticks of Juicy Fruit gum on the branches. The tree resembled Big Bird."

Chuckles escape from Reverend and all who remember the day. Lisa glances at a man sitting near the front. "Mr. Carraway, remember all the looks people threw at us when we drove to the hospital with the tree standing in the back of your pickup truck?"

In his early sixties and dressed in a navy suit, Mr. Carraway says, "Yes, a police officer pulled us over and asked what was going on." He points over a shoulder at three teenagers sitting behind him. "Tommy, Mark, and David were the ones in the back holding onto the tree hoping the artificial limbs wouldn't fall off. Although, if my memory is correct, I was driving as slow as a turtle."

"Yep, I was one of the boys." Tommy leans forward in the pew behind Mr. Carraway.

Lisa pushes a few strands of hair behind her right ear. "Once Mr. Carraway told the officer we were delivering the tree to the hospital for our friend, the policeman offered us an escort. The cars lined up in a caravan." She chuckles. "Reverend drove a minivan with a load of kids, and David's parents followed in their SUV with more youth. We thought we were cool with the police car's blue lights flashing and us following."

Reverend's eyes crinkle at the corners. "The situation was hilarious. Adults, kids, and a police officer trying to get the big yellow tree in Juicy Fruit's room with nurses and doctors following us down the hallway."

Lisa laughs and stands straighter. I see her nerves have settled down. "I thought for sure we'd lose half the gum. The tree lunged this way and that way when removed from the truck." She looks at the teens. "You guys were reckless maneuvering the tree in and out of the elevator and up and down the hallways."

"We were loud." From behind Mr. Carraway, Tommy smiles. "We scared a few patients too."

Mark and David nod.

"We lost quite a few Juicy Fruit sticks," Lisa says, "I stuck them back on the tree once we entered his hospital room." Lisa glances at Reverend and forward again. "Do you all remember what Juicy Fruit Jay said when he saw us and the tree?"

From my pew, a man dressed in a blue uniform, lifts a hand and stands. "He said, 'I must be the most loved person in the hospital.'"

"Officer Gomez." Lisa's mouth splits into a wide grin. "Wow. A long time since we've seen you."

"Too long. But that's a good thing, right?" Officer Gomez smiles. "I remember Jay's words."

"You were such a blessing to him." Reverend steps forward. "I remember you let Juicy Fruit Jay speak into your walkie talkie and let him put your handcuffs on David."

Office Gomez places a hand on the pew in front of us. "Bringing a smile to Jay's face was my pleasure."

Lisa says, "Jay suggested we put the tree in the hallway by his door. That way, anyone who saw the tree and wanted a piece could get a stick."

"He was always joyful and generous." Reverend gazes at the congregation. "No matter the circumstances."

With trembling shoulders, Barbara stands and turns toward the congregation, her face pale and etched with weariness. "He ... he said the tree would lead people into his room, and he could explain how much our church family loved him. Then he could share the love of Jesus with others." She drops her chin to her chest and sits back down, placing her head on Jasper's shoulder.

Lisa weeps. Officer Gomez sniffs swiping a hand under his nose.

The funeral is hard to witness. Juicy Fruit Jay attended church every Sunday unless he was sick. As Jay grew older, the disease progressed to his upper body and at last, to his heart. No matter what, Jay's face always beamed with a smile.

Officer Gomez clears his throat. "Reverend, if I may."

Reverend motions the officer forward. "Please, share what's on your heart."

Lisa steps back and stands alongside Reverend. The officer takes a spot behind the pulpit. "I was the one who was blessed, seeing the love you all had for Jay and the love he had for you all." He takes a deep breath and exhales. "I continued visiting Jay at the hospital. I wanted ... whatever he had. He was content, at peace. I mean, here he was a boy in a hospital bed and not a complaint in the world."

"That was Jay for you." Reverend smiles.

"Juicy Fruit Jay led me back to Jesus and my church." Officer Gomez pulls at the navy, uniform collar of the coat he wears. "Back then I was single and carefree. Maybe going out too much on the weekends, frequenting places I wouldn't ask Jesus to tag along. Oh, I grew up in church. I thought I'd return when I married and had a family." With a solemn face, he glances at Reverend and to the congregation. "One day, I visited Jay. He asked me if I'd ever pulled my gun on someone, and I said yes."

Jasper says, "He enjoyed crime shows. *Walker, Texas Ranger* was his favorite."

"He did ask lots of questions about my job." Officer Gomez chuckles. "And, he asked me, 'If you were shot in the line of duty and died today, would you go to heaven?'" The officer's face turns serious. "I thought about the question and replied I hoped so. And Jay said, 'Oh, you're a hope-so Christian.' I laughed and shrugged off the comment. He said, 'I'm a know-so Christian. Watch my eyes.' Then Jay blinked. 'That's how fast we go from living to dying.'"

"That's a great analogy," Reverend says.

"Yes, his words hit me hard." Officer Gomez swallows. "I quickly said goodbye and left the room. I didn't want him seeing me bawl like a baby. Imagine a uniformed police officer walking the hospital halls, head down and blubbering." He pauses. "I shut myself in my patrol car and wept. I begged Jesus for forgiveness and gave Him control of my life. All thanks to a nine-year-old boy in a hospital bed."

"What a testimony." Reverend claps Officer Gomez on the shoulder.

"Amen," Mr. Carraway says.

A Christian example to all who met him, I will miss Jay.

Reverend stands at the pulpit. Lisa and Officer Gomez

return to their seats. For the next twenty minutes, the pastor shares three examples of Juicy Fruit Jay's life and the difference he made in the lives of others.

Reverend chokes up a moment and continues. "As he lay on his deathbed, Juicy Fruit's last wish was for his funeral to reach anyone who is lost." Reverend motions with a hand for the pianist who comes forward. "Everyone, please close your eyes and bow your head."

The pianist plays the hymn, "In the Garden," and the gentle notes echo throughout the sanctuary.

"As Juicy Fruit Jay prayed for the salvation of his family and friends," Reverend looks over the bowed heads, "my prayer is that each and every one of you is a believer in our Lord and Savior. Here's a question for you all." He steps to the left. "Are you a hope-so Christian or a know-so Christian? Place your faith in Christ. Surrender your life to Jesus today. Please don't walk out of here lost. If you want prayer, please let me see by raising your hand."

One hand goes up and two, three, four more hands rise. Right away, more people follow suit.

"Thank you. I see you." Reverend nods. "Bless you. If you want, come forward. I'll pray with you down here at the altar."

Within seconds, footsteps sound on the mauve-colored carpet which replaced the red carpet back in 1990. Pumpkin Creek United Church has gone through several replacements of carpet over the years. Men, women, and children walk down the aisle, a few arm-in-arm with each other. When people look around, Mr. Carraway and Officer Gomez stride forward and assist Reverend with all the folks emerging around the altar. Soft prayers pour forth. Sins are forgiven.

Oh, how wonderful seeing God at work.

After people return to their seats, Reverend prays and motions for Barbara and Jasper to come forward. When the couple is beside him, Reverend looks over the congregation. "After you pay your last respects, we'll make our way to the graveyard. First, Jasper has an announcement."

"Bring her in, boys." Jasper motions. Tommy, Mark, and David walk down the aisle pulling a red wagon with an artificial Christmas tree covered in yellow ornaments standing in the middle of the wagon bed. Jasper smiles. "Reverend contacted the Wrigley Company and shared Jay's story with them. They sent us these Christmas ornaments made identical to Juicy Fruit packets." He picks an ornament off the tree. "The inscription on each ornament reads, 'In memory of Juicy Fruit Jay. Bound to a wheelchair on earth. Now walking with Jesus.' As you pay your last respects, please take one off the tree in remembrance of our son."

The yellow, ornament-covered Christmas tree stands at the foot of the casket. Barbara and Jasper stand at the other end. Reverend gestures, and folks come forward with sixty-four-year-old Ethel Louise Thatcher leading the way. Members and visitors follow Ethel Louise's path, hugging or speaking words of condolences to Jay's parents, and looking onto Juicy Fruit Jay's face one last time.

I will never forget Juicy Fruit Jay, and while the funeral is sad, believers know they will see Jay again one day in heaven where there are no more tears, no more sorrows, and no need of a wheelchair.

16

2004: YOU'VE BEEN LEFT BEHIND

I sit and enjoy the peace and quiet under the dimmed chandeliers. I need calmness after our youth group's rehearsal of their upcoming play, *You've Been Left Behind*, which will be performed in four days on Saturday night. With the pulpit and altar table pushed aside, a small sofa, chair, and end tables remain upfront. Plant stands stay scattered near the altar steps. Costumes stretch over a few pew backs. Over the past three months, the teenagers have worked hard perfecting their performances. I believe the play will be a success.

After fourteen years, Reverend is still the pastor and as involved in the events and activities at the church as ever. After play practice, Reverend and the youth directors rewarded the teenagers for all their hard work with a trip to the Pizza Palace. I marvel at seeing the younger generations—their speech, personalities, and fashion styles. Most important, seeing these teenagers blossom into godly men and women, find their way in the world, get married, and become parents, is a privilege I do not take for granted because more and more young folks are moving away from home and attending different churches.

The lights flicker on and off two times. The sanctuary goes dark. The air-conditioner's steady hum stops.

From time to time whenever a severe thunderstorm or hurricane hits the area, the electricity goes out. Back in 1954, Hurricane Hazel struck our area, and several families sought shelter at our church since their homes were flooded. Tonight, I do not hear any thunder, lightning, or rain hitting against the windows. I wonder what has happened.

I wait in the dark and minutes later, the lightest glow of moonlight drifts through the new front, glass doors and streams down the center aisle. Tiny shafts of light peek around the clear edges of the stained-glass windows. The ambiance is cozy and peaceful.

Speaking of peaceful, last year the members replaced the old mauve carpet and changed the wall color to something other than white. I now rest on blue carpet, fifth pew on the left, surrounded by taupe walls. The ladies on the carpet committee implied the color, blue, has a calming effect on people. I agree with them.

And, thanks to the Ward family, the bathrooms were updated and red brick now covers the church's exterior. Although I do get moved every time the carpet changes, things are good here at the church.

I have no idea how long I will wait for the groups' return when someone whips open the front door, stamps over the threshold, and blows out a deep breath.

"Hello." A man's voice drifts into the sanctuary and rises. "Anyone here?" With hurried strides, he moves down the aisle, bumps into a pew, halts, and twists around. "Where's everyone?" He rakes a hand through his hair, squints, and waits. He acts as if he is struggling with his next move.

He walks forward into the path of the light, and I recognize him, Coach Richard Ross. With the right hand, he grips my top edge. "Is anyone left here?" He looks upward, and with a strangled voice says, "Please, please answer me."

Why is he upset?

Coach Ross bows his head. "I'm left here."

Was he supposed to meet the youth group and head over to the Pizza Palace with them? If so, he has been left behind.

"What am I going to do?" Coach Ross releases the grip on me, bites a corner of his lower lip, and steps into my row. With shoulders sagging, he drops down on my seat. "I've lost my wife and sons." The coach's head sinks into trembling hands.

Husband to Teresa and father of teenaged boys, Rick and Tyler, Richard Ross is the football coach at the high school and attends services off and on throughout the year. From all I have heard, the coach is a good, family man.

"I missed it." Coach Ross sniffs. "I didn't believe the rapture would happen." His next words a light whisper. "I've been left behind."

No. I do not believe what I hear. Rapture. Left behind. Nevertheless, anything is possible.

If Jesus raptured His church, everyone who attended play practice tonight will never return here since they all believe in Him. Coach Ross, however, better prepare for seven years of horrific tribulations because the sermons I have heard on the topic, let me say, I am glad I am not a human.

The coach crosses both arms on the top of the pew seat back in front of him and, with head atop forearms, he weeps. Sadness cascades over me. I feel sorry for him. And me.

I will not see the youth or our church members ever again. Two of my favorite humans, Ethel Louise and Reverend, are gone forever. I will miss Ethel Louise's fiery spirit, her kindness, and the generosity she showers on others. I will miss Reverend's love for the Lord and His Word. I am alone. Coach Ross is alone. But oh, what a glorious day for the others.

Muffled words sound from the coach. "My family said Jesus could return at any time." He lifts his head and stares at the cross on the front wall.

Before I digest the coach's words, someone opens the front door and in a loud voice says, "I'll lock up the church."

Praise the Lord. Reverend is not gone yet. Relief washes over my old, oak boards.

Reverend says, "Y'all go on home. See ya Friday night for our last rehearsal." The youth directors and teenagers' voices mingle together when I hear them shout their good-byes.

Coach Ross jumps up and leaps into the aisle facing the front door. "Who's there?"

"Reverend." The pastor's voice bellows. He walks farther into the sanctuary. "Is that you, Coach Ross?"

"Yes. What're you doing here? Why weren't you taken?" The coach grips my top, armrest edge again.

When the pastor stops at the pew behind me, the lights flicker—on, off, on, off. Then, in an instant, the lights pop on, and within seconds, the air-conditioner clicks and hums back to life.

Reverend's eyes narrow. "What do you mean?"

With an index finger, Coach Ross taps me nonstop and shuffles sneaker-clad feet. "The rapture. Didn't Jesus come?"

"No." Reverend moves a step closer. "Are you okay? You look pale."

The coach stops tapping and shuffling around, slaps a hand over his heart, and breathes normal. "I thought, you know."

Reverend smiles and claps the coach on the shoulder. "The rapture hasn't happened yet." He drops the hand.

Coach Ross sticks his left hand in a khaki-pant pocket and jiggles keys. "The play's all my boys have talked about and those books the performance is based on." He moves the other hand in exaggerated motions and talks fast. "The lights went out at the house. I couldn't get Teresa on her cellphone. My mind jumped to this rapture thing. I was frightened out of my mind. I jumped in the car. Drove here. Cars in the parking lot, church doors unlocked, and dark inside." He takes a deep breath and exhales. "No one was here."

Although the *Left Behind* books are a fictional series, Reverend started a Thursday night book club with those who wanted more understanding of the end times. Believe me, folks of all ages attend and ask lots of questions.

The books are based on God's Word—the book of Revelation. Jesus will return for His church. Those who are alive, and believe in Jesus as their Savior, will be taken up with Him. People remaining behind will endure the seven-year tribulation —a time of plagues and judgments handed down from heaven. The anti-Christ will control all happenings on earth and demand everyone worship him. Those who do not bow down to the anti-Christ will be killed.

Not a future I wish for anyone.

Reverend crosses muscular arms over his chest. "Why are you worried? You once told me you're a believer."

"I ... I am." The coach gazes downward, thumps a sneaker-covered toe against the carpet, and looks at Reverend. "I have doubts. I've never heard all the stuff my family talks about, folks disappearing, judgements, and a type of mark."

"Okay, let's review." Reverend recites John 3:16. "Do you believe this?"

"Oh, yeah." The coach's eyes widen. He stops all movement. "I was about twelve and at church camp. I remember the sermon. The preacher talked about sin and how Jesus bore all our sins at the cross. He read the verse and asked for any who believed, to walk forward. I believed and went forward. I was baptized the same night." He stands straighter. "I still believe Jesus is my Savior."

What a relief. Coach Ross is a believer and will not be left behind if the rapture occurs in his lifetime.

Reverend grins. "My friend, you're saved."

The coach frowns. "Why don't I have an all-consuming peace and confidence? My family does."

The pastor settles back with hips against the pew behind me. "You're a baby believer."

The coach tilts his head. "Huh?"

Reverend straightens, turns, and picks up a Bible from the rack attached on my back and flips open the pages. He reads 1 Peter 2:2, "Like newborn babies, long for the pure milk of the word, so that by it you may grow in respect to salvation." Reverend glances at Coach Ross. "What do you think this verse means?"

The coach's brows rise. "Read the Bible."

"Yes. Definitely read the Bible." Reverend closes the Bible. "The moment you believed, you have a new life in Christ, and in your new life, you should grow. Like a baby needs milk for growth." He points at the Bible. "This is our milk."

Coach Ross stands still. The softest 'oh' escapes from him.

"When a baby is about four months old," the pastor says, "he's fed pureed fruits and vegetables from a jar. Before long, he's a toddler and eating bite-sized pieces of food. The more you read and study the Bible, pray and meditate over Scripture, the stronger you'll grow in your boldness and confidence in Christ and grow in the Word's deeper truths." Reverend gestures with the free hand. "Like a kid goes from milk to eating pizza, fried chicken, and ribeye steak, you'll see your appetite for the Word grow. You'll mature in the knowledge and wisdom of the Scriptures."

The coach nods. "Maybe I should start attending church services more."

A slight smile pulls at the corner of Reverend's mouth. "That's a start."

"I went when I was younger and through my teen years. Our pastor said we should be a good person and do good deeds." The coach places hands on hips. "I try and do that."

"That's good. However, there's much more in God's Word." Reverend's brows lift and fall. "Shucks, I try to be a good person, but I sin every day."

Coach Ross blinks. "What, you're a preacher."

"I'm human. I have a sin nature. All humans do. I fight the sin entering my thoughts. The Word tells us, 'take every thought captive.' I must read the Bible every day and keep my mind saturated with Him. So, I know God's thoughts and ways."

From my understanding, millions of humans believe, if they are good, they will enter heaven. From my years of listening, there is one way—Jesus. I thank God, Coach Ross is a believer. However, he has not heard thousands of sermons as I where he can grow in knowledge of the Bible and mature in his walk with the Lord.

Reverend tucks the Bible under an arm and points a finger between them. "We were both high school and college football players. Now, you're a coach. What would you do if a player doesn't learn the plays?"

"Oh." Coach Ross holds up a hand, palm out with fingers spread, motioning in the air. "He'd be benched for sure. I mean, we practice, and I help the players." He drops the hand and hooks the thumb over the belt in the waistband. "The team depends on each other. Over the years, I've benched or cut a few idle players."

"So," Reverend stands at his full height, "as a player, before you hit the field, did you know your plays up one side and down the other?"

"Oh yeah. My coach would've killed me if I didn't." Coach Ross' face beams. "By my junior year in high school, I was the starting quarterback."

"We need to study our playbook." Reverend removes the Bible from under an arm and extends his hand. "Spend time in the Word." He pauses, glances over the coach's shoulder, and back at the coach. "How much time did you spend studying your playbook?"

"I studied the plays every day. Sometimes, I analyzed the plays instead of paying attention in English class."

"Do you see what our Christian walk will entail for growth and maturity in faith, assurance, and confidence?"

"Yeah." Coach Ross shrugs. "I guess I doubted my salvation because," he nods toward the Bible, "I haven't studied much. My wife does. I don't pray too much either." He frowns. "I *am* a baby in my walk with Christ. I thought after I was saved all I had to do was good deeds, be a good person." He looks downward and taps me for a few seconds. Coach Ross stops and looks up. "Man, I have a lot to learn."

"Yeah, you do. I'll help you." Reverend places the Bible in the pew holder and pulls out a pocket-sized New Testament visitors and unbelievers are encouraged to take home. He straightens facing the coach. "You were misguided on Bible doctrine, and truth be told, no one discipled you in your walk and growth after you became believer."

"That's for certain." Coach Ross peeks downward and back up. "I should've put more time and effort into studying too."

"I agree." Reverend rubs long fingers over the New Testament's gold lettering. "God wants you to be a confident Christian. And consider the godly example you'll be for your sons and all those kids you coach."

"I want that."

"Me too." Reverend extends the small Bible outward, and

Coach Ross accepts the Book. "The Bible tells us to put on the armor of God. The way this is accomplished is by reading our Bible and praying daily."

"I want confidence in my salvation and Christ like my wife and sons have. I'm going to read my Bible every day, starting tonight." Coach Ross grins at Reverend. "And I'll read those *Left Behind* books."

"Good." Reverend points toward the front pew. "Join us up there for the discussions on Thursday nights."

"I'll be here, and I'll see you at the play Saturday and on Sunday for services." Coach Ross chuckles. "Unless, Jesus raptures us first."

"Wouldn't that be awesome?" Reverend smiles and claps the coach on the shoulder again. "Now, we need extra muscle around here for setting up and removing props for the play."

The two men laugh, and Reverend leads Coach Ross toward the entrance where he flicks off the church lights. The two men leave, and I hear the key click in the front door.

Locked in our church, I relax in the dark again.

The rapture did not happen. Reverend and Ethel Louise are still here. And God, through His wisdom and power, used a "Left Behind" book series to drive Coach Ross to action to grow with confidence in his faith.

For a believer here on earth, nothing gets any better than knowing when you die, or if you are raptured, you will go to heaven. A place, I can only imagine.

17

2013: GOD'S PLAN FOR BILLY WILLIAMS

The congregation claps when fifty-three-year-old Billy Williams steps behind the pulpit, the same Billy adopted by Andrew and Marie Williams years ago. I never thought the young man would be standing at the front of Pumpkin Creek United Church. Or any other church for that matter. As always, God's ways are mysterious to humans and me.

Three years ago, Billy left the pastoral field and became the Director of the Eastern North Carolina Christian Children's Home which is an hour and a half away from Pumpkin Creek and the closest children's home in our region. When Pastor Lee and his wife approached the children's home about adopting a son, Billy's connection with our church was reestablished. Today, is Billy's first visit where he will share the home's needs with our congregation. I wish Papa Pat were alive and could see how his sidekick has grown into a servant for the Lord.

"Welcome, Billy." Pastor Lee shakes Billy's hand and takes a seat in the wingback chair off to the side.

Pastor Lee became the preacher after Reverend and his family returned to Texas to be closer to his aging parents. A middle-aged runner, Pastor Lee is lanky compared with his muscular predecessor, but loves the Lord the same. Thus far, he has served our church with a servant's heart.

I remain on the left side, fifth pew from the front with the same blue carpet under me that was installed in 2003. Nevertheless, I am certain things will change soon since the topic of carpet came up at the church's last business meeting.

"Thank you." Billy faces the pastor and turns around toward the crowd. "A long time since I've stepped foot into Pumpkin Creek United Church. I appreciate the invitation to speak about our children's home. Before we go much further, where's Mrs. Watkins?"

Someone points, and Billy finds the older lady in the audience. "I recall bringing lots of frogs, bugs, and worms into your Sunday school class."

Near ninety-five years of age, Mrs. Watkins wears a gentle smile on her wrinkled face. "You about gave me a heart attack on more than one occasion. However, I see you turned out okay."

"I apologize for all my misbehavior, Mrs. Watkins. I did lots of things I now regret." Billy grins. "Do any of you remember Papa Pat?"

Seventy-eight-year-old Ethel Louise sits on me. "Oh yes. He was such a prankster."

"He was my surrogate grandfather and more mischievous than I was."

Mrs. Watkins raises a frail hand heavenward. "Amen to that."

Pastor Lee says, "You must have lots of good stories that you can share."

Billy glances at him and turns back. "God made sure I

experienced a dose of what I gave out when I was younger." With a delighted twinkle in his eye, Billy directs a hand toward the second pew on the right where his wife sits. "Pam and I are the proud parents of eight children. Our last child left the nest last spring." He laughs shaking a head full of dark, peppered with gray, hair. "And we're expecting our first grandchild in three months. I never thought I'd be calling myself a grandfather." Billy's grin lights up his face. "I'm excited. I can't wait."

The congregation claps and a few 'amens' sound throughout the sanctuary.

I have a feeling Billy will be a duplicate of Papa Pat—fun-loving and mischievous.

"Thank you." Billy lifts a hand and folks settle down. "A number of you, perhaps, remember me, my adoptive sister and brother, Sandy and Mike, and our parents, Andrew and Marie Williams. Dad and Mom retired in Florida. After Dad passed away last year, Mom moved in with us. She wished she could've been here today. She assists the staff with meal preparation and her sweet potato biscuits and cheese biscuits are a hit with most everyone."

An older gentleman speaks up. "I sure do miss those biscuits Marie provided for the Saturday morning men's Bible study." Several men in the gentleman's age range nod.

"You three kids have turned out great." Ethel Louise assures Billy. "I knew you would. Andrew and Marie loved children. I knew they made the right decision when they adopted y'all."

Preacher Poythress would be so proud of Billy as would Papa Pat. The preacher adored the Williams children, and Papa Pat would have done anything to protect them which was evidenced by him faking a heart attack.

"I'm blessed they did." Billy smiles at Ethel Louise. "Who knows where I would've ended up without the love and patience of those two people in my life. My parents were a Christian influence on me and my siblings." Billy gazes over the crowd. "That's what I'm here to share with you all today. Children in our state, in your county, down the street from you, or in a large number of cases, the child or teen next door, need your support."

After a short prayer, Billy dives into several reasons children are placed at the home—death of parents, no relatives willing or able to take guardianship, abuse, neglect, and parents addicted to drugs or incarcerated. Then, he explains a typical day in a resident's life, and the struggles children face at different age levels. The children's home thrives on a shoestring budget and financial donations are always needed, volunteers are utilized throughout the year, and there are more children needing a home than parents willing and able to adopt.

"The biggest difference you'll make is bringing a child into your home as your son or daughter." Billy turns a tad toward Pastor Lee. "How's Matthew?"

"We love our four-year-old son." Pastor Lee nods toward his wife and Matthew sitting next to Pam. "He's a great addition in our family." The pastor faces the crowd. "We couldn't have adopted him without Billy and the staff's help at the children's home."

Pastor Lee waves at Matthew, who grins from ear to ear.

"Our staff and I delight in assisting with adoptions." Billy faces forward, touches the lapel mic attached on his tie, and sidesteps still facing the congregation. "Our goal is serving the children's needs, raising them in a safe and godly environment, teaching them about Jesus, and, God-willing, finding Christian homes where they become part of a family. You all look at me now and say, he turned out fine. Wasn't always that way." He chokes up and pauses. "Sure, I joked around, but I had my share of doubts and struggles."

When Billy turned thirteen, he hit the troublesome teen years. Along with Billy's parents, church members prayed on his behalf. I watched Marie shed countless tears over the unwise decisions he made.

"God had a bigger plan for me." Billy resumes his position behind the pulpit. "I believe, He has a great plan for all the children at our children's home." He looks at Ethel Louise and Mrs. Watkins. "Do you remember when I shoplifted from Mr. Kim's convenient store?"

Mrs. Watkins nods and Ethel Louise says, "You had Andrew and Marie all upset."

I remember when I heard the news. I wanted to whack Billy on the backside. A week before his fourteenth birthday, two boys dared Billy to steal candy from the store near the Williams' home. He stole three baseball card packs, the kind with gum inside, and two candy bars. As God would prepare, good came from the shoplifting episode because He brought Mr. Kim into Billy's life.

"You see, I was hanging around guys Mom and Dad said to avoid. Back then, I was selfish, bitter, and stubborn. I thank God for Dad and Mom's prayers, the patience and grace they extended me, and the kindness Mr. Kim bestowed upon me."

Billy did not get arrested for which I am thankful because Marie, along with his younger sister, Sandy who adored her brother, would have been heartbroken. Any time I witnessed a scolding toward Billy, Sandy's big, brown eyes welled up with tears.

"God had a hand in my situation." Billy sighs. "Mr. Kim recognized me. Dad took us kids into the store from time to time when Mom needed something. Mr. Kim called Dad." He shakes his head. "Dad found me at the park with those boys, demanded I get in the truck with him, and drove me back over to the store where I returned the baseball cards. We'd already eaten the candy."

Billy did not get off scot-free. He repaid the debt to Mr. Kim over the next three months by working every Friday after school and on Saturdays. I am thankful Billy's dad cared enough and held him accountable for his actions. Through the years, I have witnessed parents getting their children out of trouble when holding them accountable for the small stuff prepares or saves the kids from bigger trouble in the long run. Over the years, I have seen teenagers involved with the wrong crowd end up in juvenile detention or worse, sentenced to jail time. Praise the Lord. He redirected Billy.

Billy rubs a hand across the pulpit's polished wood. "At the time, all I thought about was what would happen if I ended up in jail. Thankfully, Mr. Kim was a Christian man and took me under his wing. He became my mentor. I cannot count the number of men's Bible study classes I attended on Thursday nights at Mr. Kim's church." Billy chuckles. "That was a part of the arrangement he insisted upon with my dad. You see, Mr. Kim had been in and out of trouble when he was a teenager. He'd been on the way to jail when a man he had wronged stepped up and became a godly figure in his life. He did the same for me."

The Bible study group Billy attended on those Thursday nights was no ordinary group. The men attending the study had been in trouble most of their lives, and several had been incarcerated. Now Christians, these men shared details about their troubled backgrounds and what God had done in their lives. Billy learned about other people in the world whose troubles were bigger than his.

Billy grips the pulpit. "After I repaid my debt to Mr. Kim, he gave me a part-time job in the store. No glamor there. I washed the store windows, swept and mopped the floors, restocked merchandise, cleaned the food service area, and cleaned the public restrooms." Billy winces, his face twisted in a funny expression. "Let me tell you, the public is gross." The crowd laughs and Billy waits a few extra seconds before he continues. "Mr. Kim made me tough, not fighting tough, hard-working tough. Mr. Kim provided my first job which was extremely humbling." He smiles. "You parents, consider jobs for all these kids sitting in here."

Groans sound from the youth amid a chorus of "Amen" from parents.

Billy pauses until the congregation quiets down. "You know, being given up for adoption made me feel unwanted, and when I hit my teen years, I was bitter and resentful toward my biological parents. I rebelled because of that." Billy's voice turns deep and serious. "Being adopted was a millstone around my neck. At long last, I forgave my mom for giving me up and forgave a dad I never knew." He swallows. "Those who prayed for me all those years ago, thank you."

Ethel Louise pulls a tissue from her purse and dabs at her eyes. She had been a strong prayer warrior for Billy.

Billy holds up his Bible. "God's Word gives us direction and leads us on the path we are meant to live in this life, to discern right from wrong, and how to listen to His will, not our own. This finally showed me."

After the shoplifting fiasco, Billy straightened up. He was not perfect by any means and still misbehaved as any normal teenager does.

"I struggled with my calling to the ministry." Billy steps right two steps and stops. "I maintained a tough and cool image. I thought I didn't need anyone or anything. I wanted a job where I thought I'd be cool, you know, become a race car driver." The congregation chuckles. "I pushed the thought of becoming a preacher out of my mind, but you know how God is when He's working on you."

During Billy's senior year of high school, he struggled with career and college choices. Billy, a few boys, and several men from Pumpkin Creek United Church attended a men's retreat in the North Carolina mountains, and when they returned, Billy had a sense of direction for his life.

Billy moves back behind the pulpit. "A long time ago, I learned many people believe they win arguments with God. When they think they've won, they've lost." He gazes over the congregation. "Do you know why?"

A deacon near the front says, "They're not doing God's will."

"Right." Billy looks at the deacon and refocuses on the crowd. "So, did they win?"

Folks shake their heads. A few say 'no.'

Billy flashes a smile. "If every Christian lost his or her argument with God and pursued God's plan, imagine the service that would get accomplished and glorify Him." He holds both hands out to the sides. "So, as you see, I'm here. I lost the argument. And now, I'm the Director at our children's home, and I fight every day for the kids who are given up for adoption."

The congregation claps, and Pastor Lee waits for quiet. "Thank the good Lord you listened to Him."

"Amen." Billy glances at the pastor and faces forward. "You see, I get where these children are coming from. I spent time in a children's home. Today, kids are coming from places worse than what you can imagine. They need our love, support, direction, encouragement, and most of all, parents."

Billy shares that in America, close to 400,000 children were in foster care last year because of parental abuse, neglect, and addiction.

Folks gasp, and I am appalled at the high number.

Billy punches the pulpit with one finger. "This in a country where we have every convenience and resource possible."

Children without parents. My heart cries for them. If I were human, I would adopt a house full of kids.

Billy discusses volunteer opportunities at the children's home—surrogate grandparents, donations for food, coat, and shoe drives, Christmas gifts, group-home parents, volunteers for yardwork and seasonal cleanup days, tutoring, mentoring, and business or personal sponsors for each group home's needs.

"Folks," Billy clears his throat, "I ask you and your family for prayer in how God wants your help and support of our children. And please talk with me or Pastor Lee if you feel led down the adoption path." Billy grins. "I'm thankful for Pumpkin Creek's bus ministry going into the community and picking up children for Sunday school, services, and youth ministries."

Amen. Now, I feel I could preach according to the command, "Go ye therefore and teach all nations, baptizing them in the name of the Father, and of the Son, and of the Holy Ghost." The command is go, not sit here and wait. If I were not bolted to the floor, I would be out the door.

Billy glances at Ethel Louise, Mrs. Watkins, and several others in the church. "Children and youth are our future. They need a church family. And sometimes, the best family a child has is the church."

On behalf of the children's home, Billy makes one more plea. The best way folks can help the children at the home is to become parents to a child who needs and longs for a dad and mom.

Billy clasps both hands together at chest height. "Adoption made the biggest difference in my life, and I thank God every day for Andrew and Marie Williams."

I am overjoyed with Billy and his achievements, I could

burst. He turned out better than I, or quite a few others, ever thought he would. I should not have been a doubting Thomas because God placed Billy in the right home at the right time. Now, Billy is a blessing in the lives of the children he serves every day.

18

CURRENT DAY: EVERETT'S NEW HOME

*N*ow this is the life.

No longer do I sit in Pumpkin Creek United Church. After the business meeting where all the pews were voted out, Miss Ethel Louise, Tammy, and Max worked without ceasing. They pulled old church records, tracked down members from the past, and contacted historical societies.

The good news, half of us now reside in the North Carolina Museum of History in Raleigh, North Carolina, and the other half were sold to an antique store. The store owner said interior designers decorated with pews by placing one in a large foyer or at kitchen banquettes, and he knew of restaurants where pews were used as seating for patrons who waited for a table.

I thank God that He prevented Roberta "Highfalutin" Ward from tossing me into a woodchipper. How could Mrs. Highfalutin' consider such a terrible thing. In my humble opinion I, along with my pew friends, were dispersed where God intended.

Throughout the years, the Ward family contributions to

Pumpkin Creek United Church were always intended to glorify God and have been for the good of the church and community. Even though she married into the Ward family, Roberta was not as generous as her late husband, Bennett. Their son, Junior, lives in Raleigh, and when he found out the distress removing the pews from the church caused Miss Ethel Louise, he contacted the curator at the history museum.

When Junior and Ethel Louise met with the curator, she shared Pumpkin Creek United Church's history with stories, photographs, and documents. The curator was impressed with her documentation and the history of the Thatcher family which includes Ethel Louise and the story of how I came into being.

When the plan was put into action of replicating the original church, Ethel Louise volunteered and assisted the curator on the project. Because of her age, members from the church drove Ethel Louise the hour and a half to and from Raleigh one day a week which allowed her involvement in this project she held dear to her heart.

I am heartbroken over the conversations I overheard during my transition from the church to the museum. I learned pews are becoming a furniture of the past and do not fit with the contemporary décor of churches nowadays. With more than one-hundred-fifty years of history imbedded in my oak boards, several folks wanted me destroyed for the next best thing. All I say is, thank you, Ethel Louise, for preserving history.

Now, here I sit, fourth pew from the front on the left side of the short aisle, in a reproduction of the original one-room Pumpkin Creek United Church. And guess what? The conversations families, friends, and tourists exchange in here remind me of my time sitting in church, although the chats are livelier or sillier and sometimes, more argumentative than I recall.

For more than a century, I heard sermons preached on every book in the Bible, and the reality is, Jesus paid the price for sin. The folks who accept God's wonderful gift of Jesus, they will be sinless one day when they are face-to-face with Him. The others will end up in the place described as torment, eternal fire, gnashing of teeth, and worst of all, separation from God for all eternity.

Humans, please wake to the truth.

"Whew." A gray-haired lady stops at the edge of me, swipes her hand over her forehead, and looks toward a younger lady standing between a boy and girl. "I'm going to rest my legs for a moment. Y'all go on."

The younger woman looks worried. "Mom, are you okay?"

"I'm fine. I'll catch up." The older lady smiles. "Take the kids to the next exhibit. I want a minute in here because this reminds me of the church my grandpa and grandma attended when I was a little girl."

The mother and elementary-aged boy and girl stroll away from us. The lady sits, relaxes back against my seat, and thumbs through the book in her hand.

Ethel Louise ambles among the pews, rubbing her wrinkled hand along the seatbacks. With watery eyes, she pauses by my armrest and wipes fingerprints from my plaque with her sweater sleeve. She gazes at the woman. "Hello there."

"Oh, hi. I was catching my breath," the lady says.

"I understand what you mean. My legs aren't what they were years ago." Ethel Louise steps forward, sits on the pew in front of me, and turns the upper half of her body toward the visitor. "What do you think of the exhibition?"

"I'm enjoying the display. Reminds me of days gone by."

"I agree." Ethel Louise sticks out her hand and introduces herself.

The lady places her book down and shakes Ethel Louise's hand. "I'm Margaret. Nice to meet you."

"You too."

"The replica is smaller than my home church." Margaret points at the front wall and drops her hand onto her lap. "I miss seeing a cross on the wall, our plain piano, and the pews."

I recall the day two museum workers pushed me on a cart and through the entrance of the church exhibit. We entered a huge, 'S' shaped hallway where the walls are lined with poster-sized photographs detailing days gone by, and well-placed display cases built against the walls hold memorabilia, much of which I recognized.

Margaret frowns. "I miss my church."

Ethel Louise nods. "I'm glad we created an exhibit of a time many people have forgotten."

"We." Margaret tilts her head. "Did you help?"

"Oh, yes." Ethel Louise glances at a corner where a male and female mannequin are dressed in Sunday attire from the mid-1800s. She looks at Margaret. "My family has a rich history with Pumpkin Creek United Church. The exhibit was based on my church."

Margaret's eyes widen. "The note from General Sherman surprised me." She chuckles. "I didn't know he had a nickname."

I recall the night General Sherman and the soldiers strode into our church. Back then, the general was not liked, but considering the way he helped Malcolm and his daughters to a new life and released Pastor Thatcher's sons from a Union prison, I had no qualms with the man. A replica of the note from General Sherman, or as those he invited called him, "Cump," sits in a prominent place in a display case along with the Thatcher family Bible.

"I donated the photograph of Malcolm's daughters, Priscilla

and Ella. The picture was given to my great-great-grandmother, Mary Thatcher, from the girls."

"Their story is remarkable." Margaret shifts her body and motions toward a well-lit display case against the wall. "I gave my grandchildren a small chair similar to that one."

A child's rocking chair made by Joseph Everett Thatcher, Ethel Louise's great-grandfather, and passed down through the generations, sits in the case.

Margaret faces Ethel Louise. "I moved to the area and live near my daughter and her family."

"How do you like Raleigh?"

"I enjoy being near them." Margaret shifts in her seat. "Although, I haven't found a church yet."

"Does your daughter have a home church?"

"Yes. Her church is different from the one I left. There must be over five-hundred people who attend each Sunday. I feel lost."

"At times, finding a church home is hard." Ethel Louise places her hands on top of the pew's seat back and leans into the corner, still facing Margaret. "What size church are you looking for?"

"Smaller than my daughter's." Margaret gives Ethel Louise a long gaze. "I want a connection with folks my age."

"God led you to move near your daughter?"

"Yes, I'm sure of that. My house sold within a month with no hassles. I found a condo five minutes from my daughter with easy access to a grocery store and pharmacy, and I help my daughter and see my grandchildren anytime I want."

Ethel Louise grins. "You must be a blessing for your daughter and her family."

"My daughter tells me she appreciates all my help. Her husband travels with work, and I help her with the kids when he's away."

"Good for you."

"I ..." Margaret begins. "I miss my church family and my women's Bible group. We visited the local convalescent home once a week and played games, read to those who have poor eyesight, or sang old hymns. They're interesting because those residents share their wonderful life stories."

"I'm sure you miss your church. I've been at the same church since I was born."

"You have? That's unusual these days."

"Yes, it is. If I'd gotten married and had children, I pray God would've allow me to live near them."

"You never married?"

Ethel Louise shakes her head. "No. Never met the right man and, believe me, honey, I wouldn't settle for the wrong one."

Margaret laughs. "More girls should follow your advice." She taps an index finger on her cheek. "Which reminds me. What can you share about the wedding that took place in the early 1900s?"

Ethel Louise's eyes sparkle. "My father, James, is the oldest boy in the picture. We enlarged the photograph into a poster which enhanced the details."

One of Ethel's cousins provided the wedding picture of Edward and his bride, Laura White. In the photograph, Edward and Laura pose with their children, a son on each side and daughter, Martha, between the couple holding her teddy bear. Dark handprints stand out on the white wedding dress. Beneath the photo an explanation describes the none-too-traditional wedding service—a ripped wedding train, a bumble bee, and a chocolate-covered toddler.

Margaret asks Ethel Louise more questions about the photos and exhibits lining the hallway before the one-room replica. With excitement filling her aged voice, Ethel Louise explains.

Descendants of Amos Wilson donated a photograph which showed Amos standing next to the sawmill with his left shirt sleeve sewn revealing he had no left arm.

Two photographs of Leonard Gilstrap were given by a relative, the first shows Leonard holding a jar of moonshine and the second with Leonard and his mother at a church function. Leonard's mother stands beside him on the left, and in his right hand, Leonard holds a Bible.

There are several pictures of the Sanders family and, in every one of the photographs, Wiley or Ronnie is holding an animal or should I say, pet. A brief section details pork's popularity and pig farmers in eastern North Carolina and how Mr. Sanders built a family business by supplying pork to grocery stores and restaurants.

Barbara wrote the content which explained the life of her son, Juicy Fruit Jay. She provided photographs from the time he was a baby until his death. Affixed to a wall is a photograph of a youth group surrounding Jay in a hospital bed, and a Christmas tree covered in yellow chewing gum packs. A Juicy Fruit Christmas ornament is on display in a case.

Other items on display include an original hymnal from 1875, a reproduction of Martha's teddy bear with a brief history of the stuffed animal, a partial set of worn building plans from 1899, baptismal records throughout the years, and Mrs. Sarah Ward's wedding band along with pieces of antique jewelry, china, and books from the Ward family estate.

Along the walk of memory lane, pictures of the pastors and their families, who have served at Pumpkin Creek United Church, line the hall walls. Members donated photographs ranging from the mid-1800s through the present time. A family photo of Andrew and Marie Williams with Billy, Sandy, and

Mike hang among them along with snapshots of veterans who attended the church and their stories. The exhibit covers more than one-hundred-fifty years of church history.

I am blessed to have been a part of Pumpkin Creek United Church.

Margaret's eyes widen. "You've been one busy lady."

"I've had a full life and pray I'm capable of serving Him until He calls me home." Ethel Louise shifts and places one arm along the seatback and the other in her lap. "Here's an idea, take your grandkids and visit a local convalescent home. I'm sure the residents would love seeing and hearing younger kids, and who knows, you'll meet staff and volunteers who'll share with you about their home church."

"I'll do that." Margaret's eyes brighten. "Thanks for the idea."

"You're welcome." Ethel Louise's smile fades. "Friends drove me up today, and I'm getting the last of the materials we didn't use in the exhibition." She glances around. "I'll miss this place."

Margaret looks around and caresses my armrest. "I adore all the history you've encompassed here."

"Pumpkin Creek United Church has been remodeled over the years and, recently, the membership voted to replace our pews with chairs." Ethel Louise's voice sharpens. "Mind you, I didn't vote for our pews to be taken out of the church, but I was outvoted, and here we are."

Margaret shakes her head. "Chairs."

My thoughts exactly, Margaret.

"I know. What's done is done. A few members, like me, didn't want our history discarded. We worked with the museum and created this."

"Your hard work has paid off." Margaret pats Ethel Louise's hand. "Brings back memories."

"Thank you. And the pew you're sitting on, he's called Everett and was created in honor of what God did in healing my great-grandfather, Joseph Everett Thatcher."

Margaret's mouth drops open. "You named the pew after him."

"That's right." Ethel Louise gazes down at the book next to Margaret and back up. "You should read that book. Full of stories and the church's history."

"I will."

A young lady with a staff museum name tag hanging on a lanyard around her neck stops in the aisle beside us. "Are you ready, Miss Thatcher?"

"Yes." Unhurried, Ethel Louise rises from her seat and gazes at Margaret. "Enjoy yourself."

"Thank you and thanks for sharing details about this exhibit with me."

Ethel Louise smiles and steps into the aisle. The two shuffle away from Margaret and me.

I long to wrap my oak boards around Ethel Louise and give her a bear hug for all she has done in saving me. However, I know her, and if Ethel Louise has her way, she will be back for another visit.

Margaret turns and sees the old bullet hole in my seatback. She touches my scar and picks up her book, *If a Church Pew Could Talk* by Ethel Louise Thatcher. She twists in her seat and looks at the elderly woman's retreating back. Margaret stands, steps out of the row, and bends toward the small plaque on my arm edge. She reads aloud, "With God, all things are possible. Joseph Everett Thatcher. Healed of yellow fever, 1854. To God be the Glory." With a big grin on her face, Margaret straightens and watches Ethel Louise step around a corner and out of sight.

From 1854 to the present day, I have seen God work in the

lives of the members of Pumpkin Creek United Church. Although, I do not understand His ways, God works His plan in His time for His glory.

Now for me, I am thankful I did not end up wood chips spread around azalea bushes where dogs relieve their bladders.

Yes, to God be the Glory!

ACKNOWLEDGMENTS

I grew up in a church with pews and have always loved the furniture. Pews give the church interior a reverent feel, like I need to sit up and pay attention because the Word of God is of the upmost importance. Therefore, I must acknowledge my Lord and Savior, Jesus Christ. Thank You for Your direction in every word written, every door You opened or closed, and for everyone You placed in my path who made this book come to fruition. Without my Savior, there would be no book.

I owe the biggest thank you to my parents, Ashley (who now lives in heaven) and Marie Carraway, who adopted and reared me in the church and in a Christian home. You lived out the fruits of the Spirit, taught me biblical truths, and were strong examples of perseverance in your work ethic, goals, and dreams. I'm grateful for the baby boy you adopted giving me a brother, Mike. Who knows where the two of us could have ended up otherwise? But as always, God had a plan, and we are family. I'm grateful for Mike's wife, Annie, and their two boys, John Michael and Colton. There is never a dull moment with my two red-headed nephews.

God has blessed me with the most wonderful husband and daughter. My husband, Craig, who challenges me to do better each day and encourages me when I want to give up. I'm thankful for our marriage of over twenty-seven years, the way you love and provide for our family, our travels, the places we've called home, and all the outdoor activities we've tried, enjoyed, or despised. One day in my journey of "start/stop, start/stop" writing, Craig challenged me to write Christian fiction. So I did, and here we are. Thank you, Craig, for encouraging me every step of the way. To my daughter, Ashley, who is kindhearted, independent, and stands up for what is right, I admire your focus and work ethic. I'm so proud of you! Thank you for your help with social media and your encouragement. I've enjoyed every car ride to and from school and your extracurricular activities, especially when I learned to stop asking so many questions, giving you time to relax and eventually open up about your day. I've relished your company while we watched sitcoms (some more than once), every lunch we've devoured, and every shopping spree. Since you've left for college, I miss you more than any words I could ever write. I know God has a great plan for you. Thank you, Craig and Ashley, for allowing me to shut my office door and write. You both are my inspiration, and I love you with all my heart and soul!

Thank you to all involved in the Blue Ridge Mountains Christian Writers Conference (BRMCWC). I've learned so much from all the faculty, staff, editors, publishers, agents, authors, and writers and have made long-lasting friendships that I'll treasure forever. I'm grateful to Alycia Morales who listened to me and put me on the right track with my manuscript. Thank you to Sue Fairchild for proofreading, all your grammatical corrections, and showing me where I needed clarification in the story. Thank you to Rowena Kuo who loved the idea of a book written from a pew's point of view and encouraged me. And to my invaluable writing coach and mentor, Larry Leech, I am forever in your debt. Larry and I spent a few months polishing my manuscript, meeting one to two times a month on Friday afternoons at 4 o'clock.

Not my favorite time because I was ready for the weekend. He provided the constructive criticism I needed, kept me focused, answered lots of questions and asked his own, advised me on my concerns, and challenged me on the areas where more work was needed. Larry was the push I needed to prepare my manuscript for submission to publishers. I thank you from the bottom of my heart, most of all, for your guidance and friendship. God placed you in my life at the right time.

To Peggy Ellis, thank you for being my freelance editor. I'm glad we met three conferences ago and have now formed a working relationship. Your attention to detail, edits, suggestions, and clarification made the manuscript even better. Your knowledge as an editor is priceless.

Special mention goes to my cousin, Kristi Carraway Shingleton, who's like a sister to me. Thanks for reviewing my social media ideas. You're a prayer warrior I can always count on, and your words of encouragement mean the world to me. I think you were as excited as I for the release of this book.

For my two writer friends, Lynelle Lawrence Allen and Charlotte Jackson. I thank God we met at our first BRMCWC and have been there for each other through all the ups and downs of the writing and publishing process. We have become prayer warriors for each other in our writing, over our families, and through health concerns. Love y'all!

For every relative, friend, or acquaintance I've talked with about my book, thank you all for the words of encouragement and prayers.

Being human, I'm sure I've forgotten to thank someone. Please forgive me.

I hope this book encourages you to recall precious memories of days gone by, pass on your stories to the younger generations in your life, share with others what God has done for you, and grow closer to our Heavenly Father through our Lord and Savior, Jesus Christ.

If you are an unbeliever, I pray "... that whoever believes in Him shall not perish, but have eternal life."

To God be the glory!

ABOUT THE AUTHOR

Cindy Carraway Williams was adopted when she was an infant. A year later, her parents adopted a baby boy giving her a brother. They were raised in eastern North Carolina, where their back door remained unlocked, so family and friends could enter into their home away from home. Memories overflowed and stories flourished around the kitchen table especially at dinnertime, Sunday lunches, and holidays. Cindy learned 'southern' cooking from her mom, can bake a cake from scratch, and to this day, never follows a recipe exactly as written.

Each Sunday, her family attended church—Sunday school, morning service, and the evening service. Her dad served as a deacon and her mom taught Sunday school. Together, her parents served as middle school-age youth leaders. Her dad and mom lived the fruits of the Spirit, and Cindy thanks God every day for her Christian parents.

Cindy has always led an active lifestyle and that's how she knew she'd marry her husband, Craig. In their first month of dating, they participated in a 150-mile bike fundraiser where she crossed the finish line a bike length ahead of Craig (or maybe he let her). Once Cindy and Craig married, his career took them out-of-state. While living in the northeast, Cindy pursued a career in sales and marketing and became a member of New Jersey Romance Writers. She attempted writing romance until their daughter, Ashley, was born. Moving three times before Ashley was four-years old, Cindy's writing career stalled. On their last relocation, her family settled on the North Carolina coast and near family. They were back home. In their small town, her family found a church home where Cindy met two authors whose dedication to writing inspired her to sit in front of her computer and type the words God placed in her mind and on her heart.

With a love for science fiction movies and television shows, Cindy decided to write from points of view other than human and incorporate biblical truths. After her morning time with Jesus and coffee, she can be found at her keyboard working on her next manuscript or writing devotions. Cindy hopes and prays her words give God the glory always.

Made in the USA
Columbia, SC
22 August 2024